Robyn Donald

THE RICH MAN'S ROYAL MISTRESS

The Royal House of Illyria

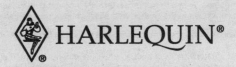

HARLEQUIN®

TORONTO • NEW YORK • LONDON
AMSTERDAM • PARIS • SYDNEY • HAMBURG
STOCKHOLM • ATHENS • TOKYO • MILAN • MADRID
PRAGUE • WARSAW • BUDAPEST • AUCKLAND

If you purchased this book without a cover you should be aware that this book is stolen property. It was reported as "unsold and destroyed" to the publisher, and neither the author nor the publisher has received any payment for this "stripped book."

ISBN-13: 978-0-373-12575-3
ISBN-10: 0-373-12575-5

THE RICH MAN'S ROYAL MISTRESS

First North American Publication 2006.

Copyright © 2006 by Robyn Kingston.

All rights reserved. Except for use in any review, the reproduction or utilization of this work in whole or in part in any form by any electronic, mechanical or other means, now known or hereafter invented, including xerography, photocopying and recording, or in any information storage or retrieval system, is forbidden without the written permission of the publisher, Harlequin Enterprises Limited, 225 Duncan Mill Road, Don Mills, Ontario, Canada M3B 3K9.

All characters in this book have no existence outside the imagination of the author and have no relation whatsoever to anyone bearing the same name or names. They are not even distantly inspired by any individual known or unknown to the author, and all incidents are pure invention.

This edition published by arrangement with Harlequin Books S.A.

® and TM are trademarks of the publisher. Trademarks indicated with ® are registered in the United States Patent and Trademark Office, the Canadian Trade Marks Office and in other countries.

www.eHarlequin.com

Printed in U.S.A.

All about the author...
Robyn Donald

Greetings! I'm often asked what made me decide to be a writer of romances. Well, it wasn't so much a decision as an inevitable conclusion. Growing up in a family of readers helped, and then shortly after I started school, I began whispering stories in the dark to my two sisters. Although most of those tales bore a remarkable resemblance to whatever book I was immersed in, there were times when a new idea would pop into my brain—my first experience of the joy of creativity.

Growing up in New Zealand, in the subtropical north, gave me a taste for romantic landscapes and exotic gardens. But it wasn't until I was in my mid-twenties that I read a Harlequin book and realized that the country I love came alive when populated by strong, tough men and spirited women.

By then I was married and a working mother, but into my busy life I crammed hours of writing; my family have always been hugely supportive. And when I finally plucked up enough courage to send off a manuscript, it was accepted. The only thing I can compare that excitement to is the delight of bearing a child.

Since then it's been a roller-coaster ride of fun and hard work and wonderful letters from fans.

CHAPTER ONE

THE CHINA on the trolley rattled a little as Melissa Considine pushed it along the wide glassed-in corridor that gave privacy to the royal suite. Biting her lip, she slowed down, hoping that the guest in the most palatial rooms in the extremely exclusive lodge wasn't a stickler for punctuality.

Most of the guests she'd met since starting her internship at this fabulous place in New Zealand's Southern Alps had been very pleasant, but she'd discovered that people who should know better could be condescending, haughty and just plain ill-mannered.

And that the staff who served them had to take all that in their stride.

'Although there's a subtle but obvious difference between rudeness and abuse,' the manager explained during the orienting session, 'New Zealanders, including those paid to serve the rich and influential, have a very good sense of their own dignity. Don't take abuse from anyone—and that includes the chef!'

A wry smile curved Melissa's lips. Her mother, who'd made sure her children appreciated the prestige that went with the famous name of Considine, borne by the ruling house of Illyria for a thousand years or so, had also been insistent on exquisite manners and true grace. She'd have been shocked out of her elegant shoes by some of the stories her daughter had heard in the lodge staff-room.

But Melissa was five minutes late, so if the man in the royal suite complained she'd be politely deferential and apologetic, even if she had to bite her tongue.

She stopped at the heavy wooden door and knocked.

'Come in,' a male voice said from the other side.

On sudden full alert, Melissa froze. She knew that voice...

The command was repeated, this time with an undertone of impatience. 'Come in.'

Melissa swallowed to ease a suddenly dry throat, and used her key to open the door. Keeping her gaze on the trolley, she pushed it into the room and stopped just inside, heart skipping nervously.

Nothing happened. After a couple of uncomfortable seconds she looked up. Her pulse lurched into agitated urgency.

Big, totally dominant, the man silhouetted against the windows didn't move. The long southern dusk had tinted the lake and the mountains behind in subtle shades of blue and grey, but he was concentrating on the papers in his hand.

It *was* Hawke Kennedy—she'd know him anywhere. Melissa fought back the feverish excitement that roared into life from nowhere.

With a decisive movement he flicked the papers together and put them into a briefcase on the nearby table. Only then did he look up.

His tough, arrogantly featured face didn't alter, but she registered the change in his amazing eyes the moment he recognised her—about a second after he'd started his cool, deliberate survey. Stupidly, she was pleased, even though she knew Hawke probably hadn't met many women tall enough to look him almost straight in the eyes—except for a ravishing model he was occasionally seen with.

Knowing herself to be far from ravishing, Melissa straightened her shoulders and said tonelessly, 'Dinner, sir.'

'Well, well, well,' he said softly. 'Melissa Considine. No, as of a couple of weeks ago—Princess Melissa Considine of Illyria, only sister of the Grand Duke of Illyria. What the hell are you doing pushing a dinner trolley two stops past the furthest ends of the earth?'

'I'm an intern here,' she said stiffly, irritated and embarrassed by the heat in her cheeks.

How did he know that her older brother, Gabe, had had his right to their ancestors' title confirmed by their cousin, the ruling prince? Illyria was a small realm on the Mediterranean coast and the ceremony had been private, of interest only to Illyrians.

Beneath lifted black brows, Hawke's green gaze travelled from her face to the trolley she'd pushed in front of her like a shield. A slow throb of sensation reverberated through Melissa like the roll of distant drums.

In a voice textured by sardonic inflection, he enquired, 'You're doing an internship in waiting on hotel guests? What do your brothers think of that?'

'I'm doing a master's in management. This is part of it.' Flustered, she folded her lips firmly together. It was none of his business what she was doing there.

Another long, considering stare sent prickles across her skin. 'Waiting on guests?'

She allowed irony to tinge her smile. 'It's good for me to find out what it's like at the coalface.'

Of course he picked up on the subtle criticism. His lashes drooped, lending a saturnine cast to his features.

In response, more colour burned along the high cheek-bones Melissa had inherited from a mediaeval Slavic princess. Reminding herself that he was a guest, she added hurriedly, 'But this isn't normally part of my job. I'm filling in for one of the staff who's ill.'

'I see.' Metallic red highlights gleamed in his charcoal hair as he reached into his pocket. 'Thank you.'

It gave her great pleasure to be able to say, 'Tipping isn't necessary in New Zealand, sir, unless the waiter has done something out of the ordinary.'

Only to recall, too late, that he was a New Zealander. The proffered tip must have been a deliberate attempt to humil-iate her.

No, she was being paranoid. Why would he do that? He barely knew her. He was probably finding his handkerchief!

Straight black brows drew together. 'Indeed,' he drawled after a tense second. 'Thank you, Melissa—or should I call you Your Highness?'

'No,' she said, without trying to smooth her tone. 'That's Gabe's title, not mine.'

One dark brow rose. 'But you are officially a princess of Illyria.'

Reluctantly she nodded. 'It's just a courtesy title because I happen to be Gabe's sister. The real Princess of Illyria is Ianthe, because she is our cousin Alex's wife.' She hesitated, then asked, 'Would you mind not telling anyone here about it?'

His broad shoulders lifted a little. 'If you don't want them to know, of course I won't tell them,' he said. 'But New Zealanders are quite forgiving of foreign royalty, you know. Your *real* Princess Ianthe is one of us, after all.'

In her most colourless tone she insisted, 'I'm not royalty.'

He ignored that. 'Tell me what an Illyrian princess—even

one majoring in management—is doing working at the Shipwreck Bay Lodge in New Zealand.'

Her head came up. 'Plenty of princesses work for their living.'

'Not usually those who can boast an ancestry as old as Europe, scattered with the names of every royal house that's existed since the beginning of the millennium.' Green eyes narrowed and intent, he surveyed her. 'And one with two brothers who have the power and money to cocoon you in luxury. So why aren't you enjoying all that wealth and privilege can offer you?'

The cynical note in his voice rocked her poise. She knew Hawke Kennedy's story—he'd left school as soon as he could, worked in the construction business for a couple of years, then made a fortune in property development in the Pacific area before broadening his financial interests and conquering the world.

If she said she wasn't interested in living an aimless, self-indulgent life, she'd just sound smug. So she shrugged and said flippantly, 'Because boredom's not my thing.'

'Very worthy.' His beautifully sculpted mouth curved in a coolly quizzical smile. 'But hotel management? I'd have thought you'd have chosen a career more in keeping with your position in society—a career that gave you plenty of time off for house parties and travel.'

'Until a month ago I had no position in society,' she returned crisply. 'Yes, my grandfather was the Grand Duke of Illyria, but both he and the ruling prince were killed fighting the usurper. The first thing the dictator did once he was in power was abolish all titles and withdraw citizenship from everyone who'd managed to escape. America granted my father refugee status, and he lived and died plain Mr Considine. I was born Melissa Considine, and that's who I am still.'

Her tone should have silenced him, but Hawke kept on probing. 'However, your brothers are now both citizens of Illyria, and Gabe is Grand Duke—third in importance to Prince Alex after his small son.'

'Alex is very persuasive,' she admitted wryly. 'Once he'd been crowned, he persuaded us all to renew citizenship, and then convinced Gabe to accept the title of Grand Duke, which automatically made Marco a prince and me a princess. It means nothing to anyone except the Illyrians.'

His hooded gaze sent an odd tingle through her, but all he said was, 'I've no doubt you'll carry it off very well.'

The practised compliment chafed her pride. Appalled, she realised she wanted much more from him than meaningless flattery. 'It doesn't change who I am, or what I am.'

A cynical smile curved his hard mouth, but he left the subject. 'So tell me why the sister of two of the most respected commercial brains in the world is planning a career in hospitality.'

Although an inner caution warned her to be circumspect, she opted for the truth—mainly, she admitted reluctantly, driven by a desire to make him understand her. 'Like Alex and my brothers, I want to help Illyria regain prosperity and peace. We can earn overseas currency through tourism, but the industry will have to be managed very carefully so that we don't lose what makes Illyria special.'

He inclined his dark head. 'Exclusive lodges in the mountains.'

'Yes.' Dangerously pleased that he'd understood, she smiled.

'It makes sense. And of course with your brothers to back you, success is assured.'

Over the years Melissa had learned to hide her shyness with a veneer of composure, but for some unfathomable reason Hawke Kennedy had only to look at her to crack her normally self-sufficient mask.

Still, she wasn't going to let him insinuate that she wasn't capable of carrying out her plans. 'Given hard work and some luck, I hope so,' she said evenly. 'Is there anything else you need?'

'No, that's it for now,' he said, an undercurrent of amusement in his tone chipping away even more of her poise.

'I hope you enjoy your meal,' she said automatically, before escaping to the corridor, huddled in the tattered remains of her poise.

Halfway to the kitchen her steps slowed. In front of one of the big windows overlooking the lake, she stopped to give her racing heart and jumping nerves time to slow down.

Fixing her gaze on the sombre symphony of mountains and lake outside, she blew out a long, shaking breath. Of all the coincidences in the world, this had to be the most incredible! She'd known Hawke for several years; he was a friend of her older brother, Gabe—although she didn't think they'd seen much of each other lately. His buccaneering good looks and formidable presence always made a powerful impression on her, but instinct warned her to keep her distance. The first time she'd met those enigmatic green eyes she'd known she'd be no match for him.

And he'd treated her with a kind of avuncular friendliness that made her feel very young and raw and totally lacking in sex appeal.

Which she was, compared to the model in his life—the exquisite Jacoba Sinclair, who seemed not to care about his occasional brief affairs with other women. Melissa had no illusions about her own looks.

A year previously she'd danced with Hawke at the wedding

of one of her French cousins. She'd accepted his invitation only because to refuse would have been flagrantly rude.

A few months before, he'd broken a young actress's heart, callously discarding her after a whirlwind affair to go back to his off-again, on-again mistress. The poor woman had tried to commit suicide, and for a few weeks her tragic, beautiful face had been in all the tabloids. Hawke had remained silent about the affair and eventually the fuss had died down, but it left a sour taste in Melissa's mouth.

She despised philanderers.

So it had been a huge shock to feel a silkily sensuous shudder tighten her skin when his arms closed around her and he swung her onto the dance floor. She'd parried his coolly satirical observations with a few inconsequential words and kept her eyes averted from his speculative green gaze. Of course he'd danced like a dream, holding her close enough to brush against the lean, honed strength of his big body, yet far enough away to tantalise a part of her into eager, forbidden awareness.

It had been a ridiculously overblown response; with two extremely handsome brothers she was accustomed to male beauty.

Yet five minutes ago in the royal suite exactly the same thing had happened again, and to her shock she realised that the lazily seductive tune they'd danced to on that romantic Provençal night was winding sinuously through her mind.

Melissa blinked fiercely, forcing herself to banish the memory of a candlelit château ballroom and the heavy, sensuous perfume of roses. She pressed the palms of her hands to her eyes, then opened them and stared angrily at the dark bulk of the mountain across the lake, dotted now with tiny twinkling lights as the snow-groomers worked.

'All right, so he's gorgeous,' she muttered, horrified to find that her voice slurred the words as though she were drunk. She dragged in a deep, deliberate breath. 'And he's taller than you, which has to be a bonus.'

Not many men were.

And *gorgeous* wasn't exactly the right word to describe Hawke Kennedy. Oh, he pleased her eyes—'Too much,' she muttered—but his boldly chiselled features were more forceful and intimidating than handsome.

Something about him set alarm bells jangling through her in primal, instinctive response. He looked like a man who'd make a very bad enemy.

Well, not precisely *alarm* bells—more a rush of adrenalin that kindled a volatile, reckless fire deep in the pit of her stomach.

His strong impact had a lot to do with his height and his powerful, athletic presence, but it was more basic than that. She'd met other men as tall without even a tingle of awareness. Melissa shivered, foolishly letting herself recall the romantic waltz they'd shared.

In spite of her antagonism, for the first time in her life she'd felt sexy and light, like someone made dizzy by champagne. Her mind had spun, and she'd been glad he hadn't kept talking, because it was all she could do to keep her feet moving and her face composed.

And when she'd looked up into his tough, compelling face she'd realised his eyes were a dark, disturbing green lit by gleaming starbursts of gold around the pupils.

That had been a year ago, yet she still remembered every sharp, astonished perception, each addictive shaft of sensation.

Which was humiliating, because when the dance was over Hawke had smiled at her, thanked her without trying to hide the note of irony in his voice, and delivered her to her group, staying to chat for a few minutes.

Then the next dance had been announced, and he'd left them. Five minutes later she'd seen him with a luscious American divorcée. He'd been smiling again, but this was an entirely different smile. Cool yet dazzling, dangerously intent, its predatory glint had made Melissa realise just how detached he'd been with her.

A fierce, bleak envy had consumed her and she'd had to look away. So of course she'd tried very hard to forget him, yet the effect he'd had on her hadn't faded; sometimes she even dreamed about him.

How stupid was *that!*

Startled, Melissa realised she was still standing in front of the window. Although darkness had finally enveloped the mountains, starshine burnished the waters of the lake, and from behind the peaks a soft glow proclaimed an imminent moon.

A perfect night for lovers, she thought, a strange desolation aching inside her.

Hawke Kennedy was as far out of her reach as any man could be. She was a virgin, for heaven's sake! If he kissed her she'd probably faint. And his type was definitely not innocent; Jacoba Sinclair, a glorious redhead, oozed sensuous confidence, as had the other women he'd been linked to, including the actress, now a minor star. Lucy? Yes, Lucy St James—and she'd better get back to work!

Guiltily Melissa scurried into the noisy, clattering kitchen, letting the scents and sounds and intense activity banish the memories.

When she finally made it to her bed she stared at the ceiling for what seemed hours before giving in and turning on the light to catch up on her required reading. But the words in her book danced in front of her eyes, refusing to make sense, so she swapped it for a novel. Even that failed her; in the end she switched off the light and lay there until sleep overtook her hours later.

And woke to someone hammering on her door. 'Hey, Mel, you want breakfast?'

'I'll be there in ten minutes,' she called after a horrified glance at her alarm clock.

She was still scrambling to make up time when the manager asked her to drop in to see him. Startled, she presented herself at his office.

'Come in,' he said, looking up with a slight frown that intensified when he saw her. 'Sit down, Mel.'

What sin of commission or omission was she guilty of? She arranged her long legs and tried to look serene.

After shuffling some papers on his desk, the manager said neutrally, 'I believe you know Hawke Kennedy.'

'I've met him before. I wouldn't say I knew him.' Fantasising about a man didn't count. Hoping fervently that her skin wasn't as hot as it felt, she asked, 'Does it matter?'

The manager relaxed into a smile tinged by perplexity. 'If it doesn't matter to you, then it's fine by me. And you can certainly have dinner with him; Lynne's over her cold so you won't be needed to fill in for her again.'

Dinner with Hawke Kennedy? Melissa reined in her astonished response. In a colourless voice she said, 'Oh, right. I'll get back to work, then.'

He nodded, but when she went to stand up he said, 'By the way, I've just finished reading your submission on the glowworm caves. You're right—they're an asset we've more or less ignored. I still don't know what anyone sees in going underground in dank, dark caves—'

'A sense of adventure,' she broke in eagerly. 'And the glowworms are exquisite. It wouldn't just be the caves—if you turned it into an expedition by taking guests out on the lake and giving them cocktails, then showing them the caves and having dinner afterwards on the boat, it would be great. Especially if there's a moon.'

He laughed. 'OK, draw up a plan. Keep costs as low as you can; we want the guests to feel that no expense is spared, but the accountants at Head Office will go over it with a fine-tooth comb.'

She noticed a certain withdrawal in his tone in the last sentence as though he'd thought better of what he said. Of course; he now had her slotted in with the super-rich world of Hawke Kennedy.

Her telephone was ringing when she opened the door of the cupboard she'd been given for an office; she made a dive for it, then had to juggle the receiver until she'd grasped it firmly enough to say abruptly, 'Melissa.'

'Hawke.'

Of course she recognised the coolly confident tone. Her stomach clenched and she said inanely, 'Hello.'

'Have dinner with me tonight.'

Why? A simple courtesy on his part? That galled her stubborn pride. She didn't want *courtesy* from him; she wanted fire and passion and flash and thunder.

Oh, why not aim for the moon? She had a better chance of getting that. And she had to tamp down her first instinct to refuse; he was a guest. Keeping her voice as level as she could, she replied, 'I've already been told that I'm having dinner with you.'

And then flushed, because she'd sounded petulant and—horrors—*deprived*, as though she wanted this to be a real date! Of course it wasn't; he was merely being polite to the sister of one of his friends. And she had to accept for the same reason.

'Sorry if that offended you.' But he didn't sound sorry; he sounded amused. 'I checked with the manager first to make sure it wouldn't upset his staff roster.'

Very considerate of him! In a wooden voice she said, 'That would be lovely, thank you.'

'I'll see you at eight, then.' Now he sounded crisp and businesslike.

Yes, definitely a duty meal. After tonight he'd probably ignore her. Not that she saw much of the guests, anyway. 'I'll look forward to it,' she said, repressing the rebellion that threatened to curdle each word.

His deep laughter was shaded by more than a hint of irony. 'I won't take up much of your spare time.' And he hung up.

Slowly she replaced the receiver.

She'd really enjoyed being at Shipwreck Bay. No one had expected her to be anything other than what she was—plain Melissa Considine.

With, she thought gloomily, the emphasis on *plain*. Love them though she did, in some ways having two outrageously handsome brothers had been a cross for her to bear. People expected another magnificent Considine, only to be taken aback when introduced to a lanky woman with strongly marked features and brown hair. Apart from her height, there was absolutely nothing interesting about her; she hadn't even inherited the famous blue Considine eyes. Hers were a boring light brown.

And she'd totally missed out on the unconscious aura she envied in her brothers. Hawke Kennedy had it too—that powerful pulse of authority and confidence, as though there wasn't anything in the world he couldn't deal with.

So what on earth was she going to wear to dinner with him? A year ago she'd have asked Gabe's fiancée for advice;

Sara had been easy to talk to, and she had impeccable taste—something else Melissa had missed out on.

However, the engagement had broken up in a blaze of publicity, leaving Gabe bitterly unhappy behind an armour of grim control. And she hadn't seen Sara since.

Think *duty*, Melissa advised herself curtly. And wear the little black dress you bought in Paris.

It was difficult to keep her mind on her work; during that interminable day she found herself drifting off into daydreams interspersed with periods of painful anticipation that brought heat to her skin, and made her chide herself for her stupidity.

But eventually she was ready. Dissatisfied, she turned away from the mirror. The black dress might be sophisticated, but it drained the colour from her skin so that the blusher she'd used stood out like two streaks of paint on her cheekbones.

Why had she never noticed that before?

Because it had never mattered. Under the tutelage of a tiny, exquisite mother, a true Frenchwoman with superb grooming and clothes, she'd learned to minimise her height and stay in the background. Until tonight she hadn't wanted to impress any man enough to worry about whether a colour suited her or not.

Or whether she looked sexy.

Disgusted with herself for caring so much about Hawke's opinion—a man who'd never given her any reason to indulge this stupidly adolescent reaction—she wrenched off the black dress and wiped away her blusher.

She surveyed her scanty wardrobe before setting her jaw and taking down a top in darkly bronze silk with fake bronze and gold 'jewels' around the V-neck. Sara had given it to her, along with velvet jeans in the same rich colour. Melissa had never worn them; she'd only packed them because she'd been told New Zealanders were noted for their informality.

So she'd be informal for Hawke Kennedy.

She scrambled into the top and jeans, then surveyed her long, narrow feet in despair. Not one pair of shoes suited the sleek jeans. Eventually she set her jaw and pulled on a pair of high-heeled boots in black.

Her mother would have called the whole outfit vulgar, and told her that the long, slim lines made her look taller. Well, she thought robustly, she didn't care. At least she looked a little more alive in it. Although that was probably because the twisting and turning of getting dressed had produced a flush in her cheeks.

Frowning, she stared at her reflection. No foundation, she thought defiantly. Her skin was pretty good, even if she did say so herself. What lipstick? Her favourite peach didn't go with the rich bronze of her clothes. She examined her lip gloss, a shade of soft coppery-pink. If she used that on its own it might look good with the clothes.

It did.

Eyes? Distastefully she examined the open eyeshadow palette. Normally she used muted greens, but tonight something compelled her to pick out a smoky golden brown and apply it with a slightly unsteady hand.

'Actually, that's not bad,' she said slowly, after scrutinising herself.

The rich colour around her eyes intensified their almond shape and gave them a heavy-lidded smoulder that startled her. It also picked up hitherto unnoticed golden highlights in her irises.

And the soft sheen to her lips looked…well, slightly provocative.

Or had she just made a fool of herself? Would Hawke take one look at her with cynical eyes and realise that she'd gone to an awful lot of trouble to make herself look good for him?

Her mother's voice echoed in her ears. *That colour's too bright for you, Melissa. It makes you look vulgar and brassy. Stay with classic colours and lines. With your height you need to be subtle, not blatant.*

Melissa took a deep breath. Although her mother had rarely commented on her tall daughter's lack of beauty and grace, Melissa knew she'd always been a disappointment.

Setting her too obvious jaw, she pulled her hair away from her face and pinned it severely at the back of her neck. There, that should show Hawke she hadn't tried to be seductive.

Stifling a familiar sense of inadequacy, she said flippantly, 'Sorry, Mama.'

But at the door she turned back, seized by a painful sense of her own inadequacy. She couldn't go out like this. It would only take her ten minutes to change back into the little black dress…

A glance at her watch told her she was running too late for that. For a second she hesitated, then set her jaw.

She couldn't face walking through the lodge and down the long, glassed-in corridor that led to the suite. Instead, she took the path along the lake edge, hoping that the serenity of the water and the mountains would calm the erratic pounding of her heart.

CHAPTER TWO

FROM the window Hawke watched Melissa stride into sight, tall and lithe and confident as a young goddess, her wide shoulders and long legs emphasising the graceful curves of breasts and hips. The glowing light of the setting sun played like a nimbus around hair the colour of dark honey, tied back to reveal the striking contours of her face.

A severe goddess, he decided—more Minerva than Venus. But then, he'd always preferred the challenge of intelligence to overt, eager sexuality.

Something stirred into life inside him, a lazily predatory instinct that startled him.

He ignored it. Desire could be inconvenient, and over the years he'd learned to manage it.

He'd known from their first meeting four years ago that Melissa Considine wasn't a suitable candidate for an affair. Apart from the fact that Gabe was a good friend, she simply wasn't his type; refreshingly down-to-earth, she exuded a simple, straightforward innocence that suggested a charming lack of experience.

However, because he never took anyone on trust, he had run a search on her during the day. Interestingly, it had turned up precious little; perhaps that innocence was real.

Or perhaps, he thought cynically, noting the subtle, sexy sway of her hips as she turned to look at the mountains, she'd just been remarkably discreet.

He could have contacted his head of Security, who'd probably have been able to dig deeper, but for some reason he hadn't.

Still, he'd found out a few things. He ticked them off as he watched her come towards him along the lakeshore. Her father had died when she was nine, her aristocratic French mother five years later. She'd gone to a top-grade boarding-school in England, a finishing school in Switzerland. With an excellent degree in marketing under her belt she was now taking her master's at a prestigious university in America. So she had a good brain—probably a first-rate one.

She stooped to pick up some small thing. Hawke's eyes narrowed and the tug of hunger sharpened into a goad when she straightened and an errant little breeze moulded the thin material of her jacket around her magnificent breasts.

Heat kindled in his loins. Damn, he wanted her…

Tough, he told himself ruthlessly. She was only twenty-three, ten years younger than he was, and she'd been sheltered all her life. He shouldn't have asked her to dinner. Hell, his one experience of an ingénue—an actress-debutante who'd developed a crush on him with no encouragement whatsoever and made a damned nuisance of herself when he'd let her down as gently as he could—had taught him not to take anyone at face value.

Young she might have been, but Lucy St James had thought nothing of weeping all over the tabloids about an affair that had never happened. He liked his lovers experienced and too sophisticated to demand any more than a passionate affair; that way, when they parted no one got hurt.

Just lately, however, he'd been thinking it might be time to consider marriage.

But not, he told himself caustically, watching Melissa stare out across the lake as though searching for a lover in the gathering dusk, with someone he'd asked to dinner purely as a courtesy to her brothers.

And that was a lie.

The invitation had been a direct result of the dance they'd shared almost a year ago. Until then she'd been Gabe's younger sister, notable only for her height, her coltish grace and her reserve.

Don't forget her eyes, his photographic memory prompted—heavy-lidded and topaz-gold, set under fly-away brows. And the mouth that made him wonder if she ever let her full lips relax into lush sensuousness.

Skin like magnolia petals, and a voice all crisp coolness on the surface but with an intriguing hint of huskiness…

Hawke said something succinct and irritable beneath his breath. All right, so for some reason she'd stuck like a burr in his memory, and that dance in Provence was still as fresh and new as it had been the following day.

Probably because he'd never danced with anyone who'd stayed so silent, practised no tricks, merely followed his lead as though caught in some bewitched time out of time!

He hadn't wanted to talk either, in case words shattered the tenuous enchantment that surrounded them that night. Content to waltz with her in his arms, he'd watched her grave, absorbed face, the soft mouth tender as though she'd strayed into a dream…

It had been an oddly moving experience, so moving that he hadn't gone near her for the rest of the night. Although, he remembered, he'd known when she and her brothers left the ballroom.

He walked out onto the stone terrace, disconcerted at his

satisfaction when she turned as though his presence had impinged on some sixth sense. After a moment's hesitation she came towards him.

Hawke drew in a sharp breath. His previous thought that she looked like some goddess of old came back to him; instead of the unsophisticated student he knew her to be, she projected a potent physical radiance.

Her smile, tentative and fleeting, banished it instantly, thank God.

Quelling the slow growl of sexual hunger in his gut, he said more sternly than he'd intended, 'Good evening, Melissa. I'm glad you could come.'

'Thank you,' she said a little breathlessly.

Once they were inside he held out his hand. 'Can I take your jacket?'

'I…Yes, thank you.'

After the crisp coolness of the air outside the room was warm, but she felt oddly reluctant to surrender her outer layer. The silk of her top felt suddenly thin and too revealing, the fake jewels obvious and cheap.

Nevertheless, she'd look a total idiot if she wore the jacket all evening. And Hawke clearly wasn't in the least interested in what lay beneath it; a swift glance revealed no emotion at all in the forceful features.

His closeness, emphasised by the light touch of his hands on her shoulders as he took the garment, produced gentle tremors of tantalising energy through her. The world froze, suspending them in a fragile bubble of silence and stillness so that her senses lingered obsessively on each tiny, heart-jerking stimulus.

A faint, almost subliminal scent, masculine and wholly disturbing, set her pulse rate soaring. Did his hands linger on her shoulders as though staking a claim she didn't dare recognise?

No, she told herself sternly, while her body swayed slightly and she had to control an urge to hyperventilate. Of course not; he was merely being polite.

And she was behaving as foolishly as a fifteen-year-old in the throes of her first crush!

He dropped her jacket onto the back of a chair. Masking her dilating pupils with her lashes, Melissa took a swift step away and tried to reassemble the shreds of her self-confidence by examining the table with a professional interest.

The staff had done him proud, setting the white damask with flowers from the warmer North Island—rich apricot and cream roses with a softly intimate perfume. Wine glasses sparkled in the light of candles, and the silver gleamed richly, burnished by the gentle flames.

'I hope you're enjoying yourself here,' she said laboriously.

OK, so pedestrian was all she could summon, but she was damned well going to stick to the conventions.

The problem was, she didn't want to, and she had the feeling that Hawke Kennedy wasn't a man who thought much about convention at all.

'Very much,' he said gravely.

A molten undercurrent of anticipation robbing her of caution, Melissa looked into Hawke's enigmatic eyes. 'I believe you went heli-skiing today.'

And could have bitten out her tongue. Now he'd think she was keeping tabs on him.

Not that he showed it. 'And thoroughly enjoyed it,' he said, a faintly cynical tone bringing helpless colour to her skin.

The guide who'd accompanied Hawke to make sure he didn't ski over a bluff on the way down the mountain had told her there was nothing he could teach his charge about skiing in the Southern Alps.

'Or anywhere. Good as a professional,' Bart had said admiringly.

Melissa wasn't surprised. Hawke Kennedy breathed the sort of competence that attracted instinctive trust.

'Interesting guy, too,' Bart went on. 'Good company, although he doesn't suffer fools gladly. You should have heard him lay into a snowboarder who thought he had right of way. Never raised his voice, but the kid came away with one less layer of skin. He'll remember his manners from now on.'

Through her lashes Melissa watched Hawke go across to a tray on a sideboard. He moved with the spare, relaxed grace of an athlete, his big body supple and strong and sexy.

Something shockingly hot and wild twisted inside her. She looked away and started to speak in a voice she expected to sound bright and conversational. To her surprise each word emerged with a husky intonation.

'You were lucky with the snow. Spring is definitely here.' She stopped, swallowed and pinned a small, desperate smile to her lips. 'The forecasters are saying that this will be the last dump of powder for the season.'

'Almost certainly. I ordered champagne, but would you rather have something else?'

'No, thank you.' Already dizzy at just being there, she watched him open the bottle with the minimum amount of fuss, and pour the wine into two crystal flutes.

Handing her one, he said with a smile made dangerous by a hint of challenge, 'Here's to meetings.'

Stop fantasising, Melissa told herself sturdily. He is *not* flirting with you. Or if he is, he probably does it with everyone, including elderly dowagers.

Especially elderly dowagers…

Acknowledging the challenge with a lift of her chin, she raised her glass. 'To meetings.'

Like her, he barely sipped the delicious liquid before saying, 'Come and sit down and tell me how you're getting on here.'

Flames shot up in the huge stone fireplace as she settled into a chair and watched Hawke take the opposite one. He leaned back like a king on his throne, and looked across at her, the austerity of his angular features increased by a trick of the firelight. Melissa felt like the logs in the fire—burning with a mixture of sensations.

Sedately she said, 'Fine, thank you.'

But that didn't satisfy him, and before long she was telling him about her experience at the lodge, relishing it when she made him laugh a couple of times. In the next half-hour she found herself settling into something perilously like ease, keenly stimulated by his sharp brain and wide knowledge. Several times she was surprised to catch herself laughing; to her bemused astonishment, she discovered that they shared a similar sense of humour.

The peal of the doorbell interrupted that.

'Dinner,' Hawke said, getting to his feet.

Startled, she realised that she'd drunk most of her glass of wine. Not that she could hold the champagne solely responsible for her heightened senses; when she heard Hawke's voice as he spoke to whoever had delivered the dinner, her insides clenched and that fire smouldering in the pit of her stomach flamed more brightly, burning away another layer of self-control.

This swift, uncompromising attraction had to be based on nothing more than his appearance. She had no idea of his character beyond what she'd read in the newspapers—that he was a brilliant, hard-headed businessman who enjoyed beautiful women.

And who had broken several hearts.

So it appeared that she was one of those shallow women who judged men by their looks. If their positions were reversed, she'd despise him. She despised herself.

Yet he was more than a handsome man. She blinked fiercely, trying to clear her mind of the exhilarating haze that clouded it. The sound of the door closing refocused her churning thoughts, and she realised with an odd jolt that while the two of them had been talking over their wine night had fallen outside, enclosing the lodge in darkness.

'I'll pull the curtains,' Hawke said from behind her.

She took a deep breath and got to her feet. 'You don't have to pull them. Look, there's a button by the door—press it and they'll close automatically.'

Before she could get there he'd found the button and the drapes swept across the windows, obliterating the lake and the mountains, cocooning the room in warmth and an intimacy that suddenly seemed much too intense.

Melissa came to an uncertain halt, wishing for the thousandth time that she had more poise, yet feeling alive in a way she'd never experienced before. Poised on a knife-edge of stimulation, she felt as though the last half-hour had altered her in some fundamental way.

Rubbish, she told herself sternly. It's infatuation, just like the monumental crush you had on that French pop star—hormone-driven and mindless.

Her mouth twisted wryly. For a birthday treat, her brother, Marco, had organised a meeting with that singer. Talk about instant disillusion!

He'd been six inches shorter than she was, and resented

every inch of that difference. Awed and worshipful, she'd barely been able to articulate, but the mockery in his eyes had stung. The only reason he'd been polite was that Marco owned a massive number of shares in the huge musical empire that held his contract.

Then he'd sworn at a fan who'd approached with an autograph book. And later that evening Melissa had overheard him describe her to a friend.

'A giraffe with no style,' he'd said scornfully. 'But one has to be polite to the rich men—and their clumsy sisters!'

OK, so she could smile now, but at the time she had been cut to the quick.

This had to be the same sort of temporary reaction. Perhaps she should have expected it; she was a late developer. Most of her friends had already moved on from their first affairs to embark on other, hopefully more satisfying relationships, while she'd been far too cautious to allow anyone close to her. Her mother had warned her against fortune hunters prepared to overlook her height and lack of beauty for the lure of access to her brothers.

She had enough self-esteem to make sure that didn't happen! But the fact that she'd never fallen in love was because she'd never met anyone who reached her brothers' standards.

Now she wondered if she had.

'Come and eat,' Hawke said smoothly.

He put her into her chair, and served a superb soup made from green peas and lettuce.

Melissa picked up her spoon and said, 'The chef will be pleased you ordered this—it's one of his specialities, and he says most New Zealanders refuse to eat cooked lettuce.'

'I'm afraid I followed my own inclination when I ordered;

I knew I'd be hungry after a day on the mountain, so I made sure of a solid, sustaining meal.'

When Melissa smiled a small dimple winked into existence beside her mouth, calling attention to her lips. Sheened by a sheer film of colour into pure sensuousness, each small smile sent reckless impulses through Hawke.

He defied any man to look at that mouth and not imagine just what it would feel like on his body. His reacted to the thought with violent appreciation not unmixed with a dangerous craving.

Possibly she'd noticed, because the dimple disappeared. She said primly, 'The lodge specialises in hearty meals because so many of the guests spend their days on the mountains or fishing the river. But because they often bring their wives, it also caters for the appetites of those who decide to spend the day in the spa.'

The soup was delicious, as he'd expected, but although it disappeared from his plate he barely tasted it; he was too busy enjoying the open, delicate greed with which she demolished hers. Did that frank appetite denote an equal enjoyment of sex?

Hawke reined in his enthusiastic body. She had an untouched air; with two heavyweight brothers he suspected that any suitor had been met with an intensive grilling that would put off all but the most determined. Even during the fuss last year when Gabe Considine's broken engagement had occupied the front pages of every tabloid in the world, little had been printed about her.

So—no lovers?

A heated pleasure caught him by surprise. Last night he'd detected a latent sensuality, an aura of unrealised—and possibly unsuspected—passion in her.

Pity he wasn't going to be the one to tap into it.

He said casually, 'How long do you plan to be here?'

'I leave at the end of the week.'

'Snap. I'm staying until then too.'

Melissa's heart jolted, and the knot of anticipation in her stomach tightened. Was that a decision he'd just made?

It was probably part of his charm to keep his full focus on his dinner partner, but Melissa found it intoxicating. Her confidence flowered, spiced by sharp awareness and his interest. She drank very little of the superb Riesling he poured to accompany the next course, a meatloaf surprisingly redolent of Asian flavours and scents, but excitement burned through every cell in her body.

Candlelight flickered lovingly over his bronze face as he leaned back in his chair and surveyed her with an ironic quirk of his brows. 'So where do you want to be in five years?'

She laughed. 'Probably working in some hotel chain to get the practical knowledge I'll need to make a success of Gabe's vision.'

'Aim high,' he advised. 'You should be at executive level by then, or managing your own tourist venture in Illyria. And I thought it was your vision, not your brothers'?'

Without hesitation she said, 'It was my idea. I don't think Gabe is quite sure I'll make it happen, but I will.'

Yes, she would, he thought, noting the determined angle to her jaw. 'Would you have thought of making a career in that field if it hadn't been for Illyria?'

She shrugged. 'I don't know. We were brought up to believe that it was our duty to help the principality in any way we could. My father never forgave himself for being out of Illyria when the prince was overthrown; all his life he did what he could for his country and his people.'

Did that include marrying a half-French, half-American heiress, Hawke wondered cynically, to keep him in the style to which he'd been accustomed? Not that it had been an ideal match; although there had never been any prospect of divorce, it was fairly common knowledge that her mother had indulged herself with a string of lovers.

He watched Melissa sip the wine, and that disturbing, rash attraction geared up another notch. She'd been brought up in a milieu where both parents had pragmatically made the best of an unsatisfactory marriage, staying together while seeking what private happiness they could in discreet affairs.

Did Melissa have the same outlook?

She looked up and caught him scrutinising her. Colour burned along her cheekbones and her tawny-gold eyes darkened. A hot satisfaction took him by surprise as he watched the muscles in her slender throat quiver.

When he looked at her with those half-closed green eyes and an enigmatic smile, Melissa's mind shut down. Summoning her best imitation of her mother's social manner, she asked, 'Did you grow up in this area of New Zealand?'

'No,' he said, and the iron control was back like a slap in the face. 'I come from north of Auckland.'

Determinedly Melissa asked questions about the country's northernmost area, slowly relaxing while they picked up the strands of conversation.

By the end of the evening those oddly tense moments had been smoothed over, although Melissa knew she wasn't ever going to forget them. He fascinated her, his incisive intelligence stimulating her into a conversation that almost—but not quite—blotted out her overwhelming physical response to his formidable, almost arrogant male authority.

But she took the first chance to get away, saying with what she feared was a too obviously regretful note in her voice, 'I've had a lovely evening, but I should be going.'

He didn't try to dissuade her, rising to his feet in a swift, lithe movement. 'I'll see you to your room.'

'Oh, no,' she protested. 'There's no need. It's not far away—just in the staff quarters on the other side of the building, and I can walk through the lodge to get there.'

'So?' he said, and smiled at her, and the urgent, driving beat of sexual attraction blazed bright and hungry through her body.

Because she didn't trust her voice, she contented herself with a half-shrug and a nod of acceptance.

The summons of the telephone startled both of them. He frowned. 'Excuse me. That will be an emergency.'

'I'll wait outside.'

'Nonsense.'

But she walked through the door into the wide corridor that joined the suite to the rest of the lodge. The lighting was muted to showcase the immeasurable splendour of the scenery, so she pretended to study the mountains while she waited.

Hawke joined her less than a minute later, carrying her jacket. 'I'm sorry,' he said, dark eyes unreadable.

'I hope it wasn't a real emergency.'

He shrugged and said obliquely, 'Time will tell.'

Instead of handing her the jacket, he held it out for her to put on. Swift blood scorched her skin and she felt profoundly grateful for the dim lights. How many other women had shivered with pleasure and heady anticipation at the closeness the small, intimate courtesy allowed?

Plenty, she thought scornfully.

He said, 'Are you cold? I'd rather walk outside than through the lodge.'

So they wouldn't be seen?

Stop this right now, she commanded that cynical little

voice inside her. He's been perfectly polite the whole evening and now he's going to make sure you get back to your lonely bed because he's a protective alpha male. That's all.

'I'm not in the least cold,' she told him brightly.

Together they walked out into the night, its spring crispness tempered by a hint of the summer to come. Melissa glanced up, startled to see Hawke scan the grounds with the swift, far-from-cursory survey of a warrior.

'It's perfectly safe here,' she protested.

'Nowhere is perfectly safe,' he told her as he took her arm. 'The world is full of predators.'

She shivered, partly because his touch fired every nerve cell in her body, but also because she knew he was right. Although she'd never been forced to endure a bodyguard's constant presence, after Gabe and Sara cancelled their engagement her life had been made hideous by importunate reporters and photographers whenever she'd set foot outside the campus.

She loved the feeling of anonymity in this distant corner of the world.

'The security is excellent,' she reassured him.

'It had better be,' he said uncompromisingly.

Silently they walked beside the lake until she indicated the screen of trees that hid the staff quarters from the main lodge. 'My temporary home. Thank you for a very pleasant evening.'

In spite of the prosaic subject, her voice sounded too low and breathy.

A breeze swept over the lake, bearing the scent of this uplifted land with it—the cool savour of green rainforest, of ancient rocks and snow, of distance and isolation. Illyrian mountains had been traversed by men for untold thousands of years; humankind had left their stamp on their flanks, wearing tracks, cutting forests, making farms. Until less than a thousand years previously these southern mountains had known only the call of birds and the sounds of wind and water.

Melissa shivered, awed by the sublime indifference of the natural world to the small creatures who thought they ruled it.

'You're cold,' Hawke said, and released her so he could shrug out of his jacket. Before she realised what he intended to do he dropped it around her shoulders.

'No, no,' she said, confused and charmed, trying to struggle free of its warmth and that sexy, purely male scent that set her pulse skipping. 'It's only a short distance—I'll be fine.'

Hard hands clamped onto her shoulders. He didn't hurt her, just showed her his strength. 'Don't be silly,' he said as though speaking to a child.

'But you'll get cold,' she protested, adding foolishly, 'And you're a guest here!'

He laughed softly, the reflected starshine from the lake highlighting the forceful contours of his face.

'Under this sky that doesn't matter at all,' he said, uncannily echoing her thoughts of a few minutes previously.

Something in his tone stopped the breath in her throat. With a stripped, ruthless smile that set her heart pounding, he finished, 'To the mountains I'm just a man. And you're a woman.'

Astonishment and a keen, fierce anticipation froze Melissa. Wide-eyed and incredulous, she watched him bend his head, only closing her eyes when she was certain that he was going to kiss her.

His mouth was warm and seducing. Unable to think, she held her breath, her lips softening without volition under the light pressure of his.

Later she thought that neither of them moved during those first seconds. She was aware of a turmoil of sensation—the comfort of his jacket around her shoulders, the heat of his mouth on hers contrasting with the freshness of the air, the subtle clamour of desire in her blood.

And then everything was consumed in a surge of frantic, almost agonised need.

Hawke lifted his mouth, but only for a fraction of a second. Before she had time to anticipate rejection he gathered her close against his big, athletic body and his mouth came down on hers again.

He took the kiss with an intensity of hunger that plunged her into a world she'd never experienced—a place of stark, raw passion that shut down everything but the primal urge to lose herself in it. For the first time in her life Melissa understood desperation.

Everything dwindled, narrowing to focus on this man and the heated, dangerous sensations his kisses summoned from her eager body. She couldn't have resisted even if she'd wanted to; her bones had dissolved and the only thing she wanted was to stay locked like this in Hawke's arms.

But eventually he raised his head and rested his forehead on hers. The sound of his breathing mingled with hers, harsh and impeded as though they'd run a marathon.

In a rough, driven voice, he said, 'If we don't stop this right now I'm going to make a huge mistake.'

CHAPTER THREE

DAZED, Melissa lifted heavy eyelids to stare into Hawke's face. His striking features were honed by hunger into a starkness that sent a *frisson* of fear through her. For the first time she understood the power of her femininity.

But that cowardly flash of fear was banished by bold, elemental satisfaction because she had done this to him.

Of course he noticed. His eyes narrowed, but his hold relaxed so that she wasn't clamped so tightly against the formidable power of his aroused body. He didn't release her entirely; against her taut, expectant breasts his chest lifted and fell when he took and released a deep breath.

'Princess, you pack a hell of a punch,' he said, his cheek against her forehead.

In his raw, intense voice, *princess* sounded like the most erotic endearment ever spoken in any language. And in his arms Melissa felt dangerously safe. Nothing, she thought dreamily, nothing in the world could ever hurt her again.

But pride drove her to unscramble her brain and assemble her thoughts into something like order. However, she couldn't think of anything to say beyond a lame, 'So do you.'

Then she cringed at her muted, shocked tone.

His voice was cool and self-possessed. 'You'd better get inside. You're shivering.'

But not from the cold! Nevertheless she made no protest when he dropped his arms, although she felt bereft, as though something precious had been torn from her.

Grimly she drove herself to step away from him, to turn on the path, to head towards the door, so acutely conscious of him beside her that she felt his presence in every cell.

Just concentrate on getting there, she told herself fiercely. You can think about it all you like soon, but now you need to shut the door on him so you can find yourself again.

Because although they had been the most sensuous, shattering kisses she'd ever experienced, she could see that they hadn't been anything so earth-shaking to Hawke. Oh, he'd enjoyed it, and he'd wanted her, but in spite of her inexperience she knew that most men responded in a physical fashion to a warm female body against them and a seeking, hungry mouth beneath theirs.

The gravel under their feet crunched loudly; every sense was still stretched to its limit, so that her ears picked up the hushed lap of water against the lakeshore, and her skin tingled at the soft wind on her face.

She could taste Hawke on her lips, and her tongue, and her body was hot and eager, every nerve throbbing with frustration.

At the doorway he said abruptly, 'I'm leaving tomorrow.'

A kind of sick panic hollowed out her stomach. She bit back the words that threatened to tumble out and betray her.

Squaring her shoulders, she said in a voice that she hoped sounded nothing more than amused, 'Not on my account, I hope.'

'No,' he said, his tone echoing hers. 'The phone call just before we left.'

An excuse, but nicely done.

Melissa's head weighed heavy on her neck as she nodded. 'I know about emergencies—my brothers Gabe and Marco spend a lot of time dealing with them,' she said, forcing a wry note into the words. She turned and held out her hand, hugely relieved when it didn't waver. 'Goodbye. I hope yours turns out to be not too big a problem.'

He took her outstretched hand with a humourless smile. 'So do I,' he said, and hauled her into his arms.

For a second he looked down into her startled face, his eyes gleaming in the most basic of challenges before he bent and kissed her again, claiming her mouth with hard, fierce possessiveness.

Eventually he lifted his head and gave her a narrow, dangerous look. 'This isn't goodbye, Melissa.'

She gazed into his smouldering eyes and felt her heart tumble endlessly in space, infinitely joyous because Hawke wanted to see her again.

'Then safe journey,' she managed.

'I'll catch up with you soon.'

Cold, reliable common sense returned to blot out her anticipation with uncompromising logic. She shrugged out of his jacket and held it out, knowing in her innermost heart that his vague promise—if that was what it was—meant nothing. However much he'd enjoyed those few kisses she was no sophisticated beauty, not at all the sort of woman Hawke would pursue.

When he took the jacket she managed a smile. 'Goodbye,' she said again, and turned and let herself inside, moving quickly because if she stayed he might see the desolation in her eyes.

For the rest of the week Melissa waited for him to come back. Of course he didn't, and after days of echoing silence and slowly fading hope she told herself desperately that it was all for the best.

Kisses meant little, except that her response had been embarrassing enough to send him running. Her heart wasn't broken—slightly cracked, maybe, but still intact; sinking into a decline like a gently-bred Victorian maiden simply wasn't an option to a woman of the twenty-first century.

And the erotic dreams that ambushed her in the night were just figments of her sex-starved imagination.

Viewing the situation sensibly, she should be glad she'd learnt something more about the complexity of relationships—if dinner and a few kisses could be called a relationship!—between men and women.

With a last glance at the mountains, she settled back into her seat on the plane. Half an hour from now she'd have left behind her time at the lodge, with its memories of a job she'd enjoyed and a man she'd never forget. She thought bleakly that she now understood what had led her tough brother Gabe into his catastrophic affair with Sara Milton.

Sex had a lot to answer for!

The plane banked, turned away from the lakes and the mountains and set a purposeful course for the North Island. Melissa closed her eyes and tried to convince herself that Hawke's kisses had *not* changed her fundamentally, as though he had the power to alter her basic cellular construction.

The thought was utterly ridiculous.

So she wouldn't consider it. She'd sink herself into her life and not ever think of him again.

But first she'd have a week in Northland, a long, narrow peninsula thrusting towards the tropics, where spring was edging into summer and white beaches warmed under a hot sun.

'Why?' Gabe had demanded when she'd rung him the previous night.

'*You* might be able to work twenty-four hours a day, seven

days a week, but I can't. I'm taking time out to collate my notes for the paper I'm doing on the internship while the whole experience is fresh in my mind.'

'You could go to the house in Honolulu.'

'I want to see a bit more of New Zealand. I've been told Northland is just as stunning as the southern lakes district, but in an entirely different way.'

'It is.' He sounded resigned. 'Where will you be staying?' She told him the name.

'That sounds like a backpackers' lodge.'

'It is, but an upmarket one—I've reserved a room to myself.'

'If you need money I'll organise—'

She broke in without compunction. 'You were the one who decided that I should live on my allowance. And you were right—it's not only extremely good for me to stick to a budget, but I also enjoy doing it. I'm fine, Gabe, don't fuss.'

After a moment's silence, he said reluctantly, 'New Zealand's safe enough, I suppose, but take care.'

'I always do,' she said, smiling.

'E-mail me the address,' he commanded. 'And your room number.'

'Yes, *sir*!'

He laughed. 'All right, I know you're a big girl now. Have fun.'

Sometimes big brothers—even adored ones—could be a darned nuisance, but although their protectiveness rubbed her independence the wrong way, neither Gabe nor Marco would ever change.

The little town of Russell in the Bay of Islands was busy with tourists and holidaymakers drawn to the region by its rich history, both Maori and European, and its beauty. Built along a beach, its small wooden houses were constrained by hills covered in dark, vigorous forest that Melissa knew was always referred to as 'the bush'. Neither the vegetation nor the setting reminded her in the least of Hawke Kennedy.

No memories here.

In her small, sparsely furnished room she set up her laptop on the desk and settled down to work. For the next two days she resisted the temptations of cruises with dolphins, of sight-seeing and diving, of wine and heritage tours. Every evening she went for a walk along the beach then up a steep hill topped by a flagpole.

And every night in bed she lay awake staring into the darkness.

Soon she'd be over this undignified infatuation. It was just a matter of refusing to surrender to it; she was being obsessive and stupid and girly, but at least no one else knew how silly she was.

The third morning bloomed in soft, fresh splendour, the sun beaming down from a sky so blue and bright it made her blink. However, a tentative dabble in the sea convinced her that it was too cold to swim, so she celebrated the good weather with breakfast at the café along the road and settled down with her notes.

Towards midday she pushed them aside and got up to stretch. 'A walk,' she said out loud. 'I need a walk before lunch.'

She craved solitude, so of course she met a family on the beach—a smiling, vociferous group who engulfed her when she snatched one small daughter out of the way of a particularly boisterous wave. Tourists from Peru, they sorted out into a middle-aged couple, their very handsome son called Jorge, and a married daughter with her husband and two enchanting little girls.

Melissa knew she wasn't looking her best; unlike the

South American women she hadn't bothered with make-up that morning, and she'd set out without changing her T-shirt and jeans.

Not that it seemed to matter. Jorge gave her a dazzling smile and fell in beside her as they began to move along the beach. By the time they'd reached the other end of the bay he'd invited her to lunch with them at one of the restaurants, an invitation eagerly seconded by his mother.

Her first instinct was to refuse, but why not? Defiance mightn't be a pretty emotion, but it was better than a nagging sense of humiliation. She was tired of her constant fixation on Hawke. This cheerful, noisy family would keep the useless memories at bay for an hour or so.

So she said, 'That sounds lovely—thank you very much.'

The Lopez clan wouldn't hear of her leaving them to change her clothes for something a little more elegant.

'No, no,' the *señora* said briskly. 'Here is very casual, so we all wear our beach clothes.'

Melissa hid a smile. Their beach clothes had been bought, she was sure, in the most elegant boutiques in Lima. Beside them she must look a peasant.

Lunch was protracted and happy and delicious, and by the end of it the children were sweetly nodding and Melissa also was ready for the siesta that so clearly beckoned the rest of the family.

They insisted on escorting her back to the lodge, then waved goodbye and trooped off in the direction of their hotel. The son lingered, however, just inside the gate.

'Perhaps you would like to have dinner with us also?' he suggested, examining her with such open interest and pleasure that a tinge of heat coloured her cheeks.

Melissa was opening her mouth to refuse tactfully when a voice from behind her said, 'I'm afraid that won't be possible.'

The deep, even tone displayed no emotion whatsoever, but each word was buttressed by steel. Heart jumping, Melissa turned to meet eyes as green and cold as glacier ice. Hawke, she thought, and a wave of pure happiness overwhelmed her.

The South American looked from her face to Hawke's; with a wry smile he said courteously, 'But of course. It has been a pleasure meeting you, Melissa.'

And symbolically relinquishing any claim to her, he gave a slight bow and turned away.

Struggling to control her wayward heartbeat, Melissa asked crisply, 'You had no right to refuse an invitation for me.'

Hawke lifted an arrogant eyebrow. 'Then go after him.'

'I will not,' she returned, furious yet wondering whether he was jealous. Or overly possessive. 'I was about to refuse him myself. And this is the second time you've gone over my head.'

Silence burned between them, taut and filled with unspoken emotions. All she could think of was that if only she'd known he was coming she'd have worn clothes that suited the occasion. Festival gear, she thought with a touch of hysteria, because skyrockets were exploding in the pit of her stomach and she was sure she could hear fairy music—dangerous, seductive, wildly irresistible—in her ears.

Hawke didn't pretend not to understand what she was referring to. 'At Shipwreck Bay I consulted the manager before I asked you to dinner because I thought you might have been working again that night,' he said coolly. 'As for today—you're perfectly correct, I had no right to answer for you. I'm sorry.'

'I should think so.' She angled her chin at him. 'Not that it's any of your business, but I met the whole family—mother, father, sister and husband as well as Jorge, plus two sweet little girls—late this morning and had lunch with them all. What are you doing here?'

This time both straight brows went up. In a voice that held more than a little impatience he said, 'I came here because you're here. Why the devil did you leave Shipwreck Bay?'

A car started up with a series of minor explosions that effectively killed the fairy music. Woodenly Melissa said, 'I told you I was due to leave at the end of the week.'

'And I told you I'd be back.' He frowned down at her. 'Why didn't you wait?'

'You didn't ask me to, which was another assumption,' she said, much more calmly than she felt. Anticipation pierced her, and an exhilarating pleasure. 'How did you find me?'

Narrow-eyed, he said harshly, 'If you hadn't booked this place through Shipwreck Bay Lodge I might not have.'

'I know that judicious amounts of money, carefully targeted, can buy almost anyone, but I'd have thought the staff at the Bay would show some loyalty.'

He gave a short, mirthless laugh. 'They did. I own Shipwreck Bay.'

Stunned, she said, 'You *what*?'

'I thought you knew.'

'No.' She drew in a sharp breath, wondering why it was important to convince him of that. 'No,' she repeated, 'I didn't know.'

Did he believe her? Or did he think she'd wanted him to run after her as some kind of sick, thoughtless ploy to keep him interested? It was impossible to tell from his expression; he was an expert at hiding his thoughts and his emotions.

And what, she wondered feverishly, did he want from her? She didn't even know how to ask. If only she had some idea of how this game between the sexes was played.

Without thinking, she blurted, 'Do you own this one too?'

'No.' He gave her an edged smile that reinforced the flinty

note in his voice. 'I have a house a few kilometres away. Is Northland living up to your expectations?'

'It's glorious.' She sent him a sideways glance and finished demurely, 'But I suppose you prefer the mountains.'

Hawke wondered if she had any idea just how provocative he found those occasional slanting glances—the flash of topaz fire between the thick lashes, and the tiny smile that accompanied each one.

He didn't think she did, and he wasn't going to tell her. It had taken all of his self-control to tamp down the swift anger that had roared out of nowhere when he'd seen her smile at the good-looking South American boy. He'd wanted to grab the kid, shake the greedy grin off his handsome face and hurl him out of sight—a reaction that startled and appalled him.

He said coolly, 'Because I'm rough and hard and craggy?'

The comment surprised a chuckle from her. The vagrant dimple appeared for a second at the corner of her wide mouth. 'I hadn't exactly thought of it like that. I suppose because they're more of a challenge.'

Always totally in control of both his body and his emotions, it pricked his pride that somehow this woman had the power to shake his armoured self-sufficiency.

Before he'd met her, he'd expected a female version of her brothers—younger, of course, but self-confident, poised, completely assured. Instead she'd been endearingly reserved almost to the point of shyness, although he'd seen no sign of that when she'd been chatting to the South American boy.

Was she playing a game with him? He could read most women, but this one, in spite of her seeming openness, was intriguingly enigmatic.

And the fact that she kissed like a tantalising mixture of angel and devil further confused the issue. When he'd got back to Shipwreck Bay and found her gone, he'd been furious enough to decide to find out just what made Princess Melissa Considine tick.

He said abruptly, 'The bay might look beautiful and serene, almost placid, but it can be as dangerous as any mountains.'

A note in his voice sharpened her attention. Was that a warning? She hurried into speech. 'I know—appearances are deceiving. Illyria has a big central lake, and the storms there can be furious and deadly. What are these bushes—the ones with the sharp little leaves and spicy smell?'

'Manuka trees—tea tree, we call them, since the first European settlers brewed tea from the leaves. The taller ones with softer, feathery leaves are kanuka—same family.'

She said the names carefully, adding, 'And the ones that grow by the beach—the big, dome-shaped ones?'

'Pohutukawa. In the summer, just before Christmas, they're covered in flowers.' Hawke examined the line of trees marching down the waterfront, separating the road from the curved sandy beach. 'They look like massive scarlet or crimson ice-cream cones.'

'Oh, so romantic,' she jibed.

He smiled to devastating effect. 'I'm not romantic,' he said, his tone indicating clearly that he was making a point.

'Neither am I,' she shot back, keeping her eyes on the pohutukawa tree. 'Do these trees grow only in the north? I didn't notice them in the South Island.'

'They need warmth; they don't flourish much further south than halfway down the North Island, and they like to have their roots splashed by the sea.'

'Say their name again.'

'Pohutukawa.'

She made an attempt at it, and laughed when she failed.

'Maori is a very musical language,' she said ruefully, 'but some of the words are difficult.'

'Not at all. The vowel sounds are the same as Italian, and each syllable is pronounced separately.'

Frowning slightly, she said, 'Po-hu-tu-ka-wa.'

She looked up at him for confirmation, only to see his intent gaze on her lips. Excitement pulsed through her, coloured her cheeks, lifted the tiny hairs on her skin. His eyes narrowed into glittering green-gold gems.

Melissa's mouth dried. More than anything she wanted to lick her lips, but instinct warned her that if she did she'd be making an invitation he wouldn't turn down.

In a husky little voice she prompted, 'Is that how it's pronounced?'

On a raw, driven note, he said, 'Perfect.'

To her intense and furious disappointment a woman walked past. Small and slender, she was everything, Melissa realised glumly, that she wasn't—beautiful, graceful and superbly dressed in white linen trousers and a striped little blue-and-white shirt that gave her a nautical air and dipped invitingly over high breasts.

And it didn't help that her eyes passed over Melissa with dismissive speed before settling on Hawke. Whoever the unknown woman was, she made her interest obvious with one sultry glance and a swift, provocative smile that showed off lusciously coloured lips.

'Good afternoon,' the newcomer said in a huskily sensuous tone as she went by, hips swaying, elegant back somehow sinuously inviting, her white-blonde cascade of hair swinging.

Blank-faced, Melissa forced down an alarming envy and glanced at Hawke. As always, his face gave nothing away.

'Too many people here,' he said coolly. 'Come on, let's go.'

'Go? Where to?'

'I'll show you my house.' He indicated a four-wheel-drive parked by the kerb. 'That's my vehicle.'

Another assumption. 'Are you asking me?' she said crisply.

He lifted a quizzical brow. 'Yes, princess, I'm asking you.'

Melissa knew she should say no, but she nodded and got into the car, her thoughts torn between sheer, primitive delight because he was here, and a bleak conviction that she was reading this whole situation wrong.

Hawke Kennedy could have any woman in the world, so why on earth would he choose someone without an ounce of style when magnificent sirens like the woman on the pavement ogled him?

He startled her by saying, 'What are your plans for this interlude?'

Surely he didn't mean—no, of course he wasn't asking what she wanted from their time together. She took in a tight breath and said in her most prosaic tone, 'I'm getting my notes together for the paper I'm doing on my internship.'

'What's your premise?'

She told him, expecting no more than a superficial interest. But he asked a question that made her think, and by the time they reached a gateway set in the bush they were immersed in discussion.

The gates swung open and Hawke turned the car down a drive that dipped between a stand of tall coastal forest to cross a little stream before winding up another hillside. The shade was refreshing after the glare of the sun; Melissa fell silent, wondering what on earth she was doing here.

And why had he come?

The butterflies in her stomach had increased to thousands by the time the vehicle drew up in a paved courtyard. Hawke parked it beneath another large, unknown tree, and got out. Melissa scrambled down and surveyed the house. Long and low, it was tucked into the bush, yet she could smell salt, and hear the crash of waves.

'Coffee?' he asked as they walked inside.

She shook her head. 'No, thank you, but a glass of water would be wonderful.'

'I think I can do a bit better than that,' he said drily, opening a door into a huge, light-filled room. 'I'll get you some juice.'

The entire side of the room was open, its wood-framed glass doors pushed to each end so that nothing but the edge of the terrace stood between her and a limitless view of sea and sky.

'Oh,' Melissa breathed, lost in delight.

CHAPTER FOUR

'GO OUTSIDE and look,' Hawke said. 'I'll bring your drink.'

The house had been built on the ridge-line of a steep, bush-covered slope that ended in a bow-shaped beach, its pink sand darkened by the waves. Melissa recognised a massive tree shading one end of the terrace as a pohutukawa. More were scattered over the slope, but unlike the backpackers' lodge Hawke's house didn't look over the islands and sheltered waters of the inner bay. Instead an infinity of sea stretched without hindrance in a mingled multitude of silvery-blues and turquoise shading to a barely discernible horizon.

Face alight, Melissa turned, some atavistic inner sense warning her that Hawke was walking silently through the open doors. 'This is utterly beautiful,' she breathed. 'So many colours, yet they add up to a perfect blue.'

'The same colour as the Considine eyes.' He handed her a glass of lime juice and held her gaze with his. 'Why don't you have them?'

Embarrassed by his scrutiny, she fumbled for some sophisticated response. 'They're a male inheritance. The family runs to sons rather than daughters, but the women have more choice in eye colour.'

'I believe you're the only Considine woman left now.'

'Perhaps,' she said as noncommittally as she could.

His brows drew together. 'What did I say?'

Well, it wasn't exactly a secret. 'The man who usurped power in Illyria and killed our grandparents was a Considine, a very distant cousin. Rumours say he married and had children—two daughters.'

She stopped, and he said quietly, 'What happened to them?'

'No one knows.' She shivered. 'If they did exist, they're probably dead. People in his inner circle tended not to survive long.' Ruthlessly she dragged the subject back to the scenery. 'There's nothing between here and South America, is there?'

'Nothing. Have you ever been there?'

'The furthest south I ever got was Mexico, which I loved.' She sipped some of the sweetly tangy lime juice and revealed, 'Most of my travelling was done with my mother, and she wasn't an adventurous tourist. She only liked what she called civilised places, and since her idea of civilised meant Europe and the eastern seaboard of America, that was it for me.'

'Is there any particular place you'd like to go in South America?'

'Machu Picchu,' she said promptly. 'And the Iguaçú Falls.'

He'd been to both, of course, and as they drank the juice he told her about them, his deep voice with its intriguing sexy rasp bringing each place to life.

'They sound wonderful,' she breathed enviously.

'But you can go wherever you like now,' Hawke said, his gaze intent.

She shrugged. 'I've been busy since I left school. I had a fabulous gap year in Thailand teaching English in a school, and I've stayed with friends in various holiday spots, but I spend vacations working for Gabe and Marco, whichever one can find me a job.'

He leaned back against the balustrade and examined her face with cool, half-closed eyes. 'Ah, the curse of a fat trust fund and two protective brothers,' he said, his tone laced by irony.

Well, he might as well know.

'I don't have any money of my own,' she informed him. 'Gabe and Marco make me an allowance.'

'That seems remarkably old-fashioned of your parents,' Hawke remarked, his objective tone at variance with the keenness of his scrutiny.

'They knew my brothers would look after me.' And because that sounded wrong she added swiftly, 'If I ever needed it.'

Hawke nodded. 'But in the meantime you're dependent on them?'

'Until I start earning my own money, yes.' No one would know from her tone that she found the dependency irksome, or her brothers' attitude a little too protective.

Well, Gabe's, anyway. Marco was more inclined to let her have her head.

And she was overreacting; Hawke's interest in her wasn't financial—not like the various other men who'd thought she had her own fortune. However, Gabe and Marco wielded enormous power beyond the purely financial. There could be other reasons for him to pursue her.

It hurt, but she had to face it. Once, with a sympathetic hug, her mother had told her that her face wouldn't launch one ship, let alone the thousand attributed to Helen of Troy. Men weren't ever going to fall madly, passionately in love with her.

Not that Melissa had been grateful then for her mother's brutal pragmatism, but she had since. Her only foray into love had died before it got off the ground when she'd found out that the man was actually in love with the prospect of being close to the Considine brothers. The scion of an aristocratic family, he'd seen it as a quick way to repairing the fortune his ancestors had wasted.

So did she find Hawke so attractive because he clearly wasn't looking for money or influence?

One glance dispelled *that* crazy idea. The sun shone down on his black head, lighting up the strong framework of his face with loving intensity. Fingers curling, she recalled the texture of the skin over his jaw, made sexy by the soft friction of his beard. Her heart skipped a beat at the sensuous memory, and her glance lingered on his mouth, its sculpted contours redeemed from pretty-boy perfection by more than a hint of ruthlessness.

Deep within, some previously inviolable refuge melted in a sweet ache of desire that made her dizzy. She set her teeth and fought it back, her mouth tightening into severity.

Putting things in the most basic way, she lusted after him.

Yes, she was wary, but she had few and very frail defences against Hawke's brand of potent sex appeal. If he turned up the heat she suspected she'd melt into his arms, wary or not. So he had to understand she had no money and no influence with her brothers.

He lifted his glass to her and said, 'Here's to a good degree and independence.'

'I'll drink to that,' she said, wondering if he'd now fabricate an excuse to leave the Bay of Islands.

Draining her glass, she set it down on a table and looked around with dimmed pleasure. In her brightest tone, she said, 'And I'm not going to achieve either if I don't get back to work. Have you anything planned for this afternoon? There's no chance of heli-skiing, but a group at the backers' lodge were raving about the paragliding.'

'I'm going to work too. If you'd like, we'll have dinner here. If not, there are plenty of excellent restaurants.' He waited for two beats of her heart before adding, 'That's if you want to have dinner with me.'

His lazy smile reminded her of her demand that he stop making assumptions about her.

Resolutely reining in a leap of anticipation, Melissa stole a look at him from beneath her lashes. As usual, she couldn't tell what he was thinking, although she noticed a glint of amusement in his eyes. Did he really want to have dinner with her, or was he just putting the best face on the situation now that she'd told him she wasn't going to be a pawn in an unknown game?

Did it matter? She hesitated, torn by conflicting desires. Lust she could deal with; love was a much more dangerous emotion, one she didn't dare leave herself open to. Then a surge of rebellious challenge made up her mind. Of course she could have dinner with him without losing her heart.

'I'd enjoy that,' she said steadily, and rose to her feet. 'The lime juice was lovely, thank you. And this place is beautiful.'

He straightened up. 'I'm glad you like it.'

She cast a final glance around the fantastic view. 'It reminds me a bit of Greece, only without the crushing weight of history.'

She flushed, because spoken out loud the words sounded ridiculous. Hastily she added, 'Of course, New Zealand is just as old as Greece, but it feels fresher—untamed, yet somehow innocent.'

Her colour deepened; that sounded even more pretentious.

Hawke said, 'I don't think any place with human inhabitants is free from that weight of history, but I know what you mean. I could always understand why the early European explorers were so bemused by the islands in the Pacific. In the Mediterranean the legacy from the past is inescapable, whereas here there's only a thousand years of death and betrayal and misery.'

'And love and happiness and laughter too,' she protested. 'Not all history's depressing.'

'Don't you think that there's something bittersweet about past happiness? Although I suppose your heritage has accustomed you to the grip of the past.'

'I suppose it has,' she said slowly, walking beside him into the house. 'In a way, we take it entirely for granted. Alex is sure that the Illyrians will decide to become a republic quite soon, but I don't think so—they adore him, and when his son was born there were bonfires in the hills and dancing and feasting as though the birth of an heir was a huge weight off their shoulders.'

She relaxed, feeling oddly in tune with him. Too relaxed, perhaps, because as she walked into the house she managed to catch the toe of her sandal on the step and trip.

Before she hit the floor Hawke grabbed her, hauling her upright. 'Are you all right?' he demanded, turning her so that he could scan her face.

'Yes—sorry, I'm such a klutz,' she babbled, mortified. 'I forgot that there was a step there.'

She stuttered into silence, tension spiralling between them when she watched Hawke's eyes light with smouldering green fire in the suddenly more prominent framework of his face.

Compelling, purposeful, his gaze fell on her mouth, and she was consumed by craving, a need so intense and desperate that every thought fled her brain.

Slowly, perhaps giving her time to object, he pulled her

close. Melissa couldn't think—didn't want to think. She lifted her face in innocent supplication, and smiled.

He said her name, the syllables grating across her ears. His arms tightened around her in a bone-cracking grip, but although she wanted him so much it must have blazed forth from her face, he didn't kiss her. Instead he looked into her eyes as though seeking an answer to an unknown question.

What he saw must have passed some hidden test, because he said in that thick, harsh voice, 'Princess, you set me on fire.'

And kissed her.

This time there was no holding back, nothing tentative. He demanded—and so did she, her body singing with reckless passion as embers that had been smouldering since the last time he'd touched her exploded into vibrant flame.

Looping her arms around his neck, she surrendered to her passionate craving, consumed by shuddering delight when his kiss invaded her mouth. The feverish excitement beat higher; when he lifted his mouth she heard a gasping moan and realised it came from her, and the little sob that followed was hers too, as his teeth closed gently on the juncture of neck and shoulder. The tiny, primitive assault sent an erotic charge through her, and some hitherto dormant instinct turned her head so that she could do the same to him.

He tasted of salt and musk, of delicious male heat, and his skin was fine as glove leather, sleek and firm over the muscle beneath. Transfixed, she savoured him like the finest of wines, delighted with the freedom of being able to touch him.

He laughed, the sound muffled in his chest, and moved one hand purposefully from her back to her breast. Melissa's breath locked in her throat; she leaned back a little to give him easier access, and he kissed the length of her throat, his mouth lingering over the vulnerable hollow at the base where her pulse rioted.

His thumb brushed the pleading, urgent tip of her breast, back and forth, back and forth, a tiny sensual caress that sent arrows of desire twisting deep into the pit of her stomach.

Wordlessly, she looked up into eyes lit by golden flames. Her lashes drifted down, heavy with the force of her longing and the untamed clamour of her senses. Something was building inside her, something summoned into life by Hawke's touch, by his nearness, by his unashamed carnality, and she was going to yield, to experience his lovemaking because she couldn't find the will to resist him—or her own body.

Hawke slid the material of her T-shirt up, stroking the flat width of her midriff as though he loved the feel of it. A delicious lassitude drained the energy from her bones.

She shivered, and instantly he said, 'Are you cold?'

'No,' she denied in a husky, cracked little voice, then, 'Yes.'

'So what can we do about it?'

She leaned her forehead onto his shoulder and summoned the courage to slip her hands beneath his shirt, touching him the same way he was touching her, unhurriedly, sensuously, her fingertips luxuriating in tactile pleasure.

He said her name, and when she didn't answer said roughly, 'Melissa. Tell me now, before this goes any further, that you know what you're doing.'

Know what she was doing? Of course she did. The drugging fumes of desire that clouded her brain hadn't made her stupid.

'We're making love,' she said, her voice slow and wondering, her body alight with the joy of it, the unexpected helpless pleasure.

'Ah, so that's it,' he said, a note of laughter in his voice. 'Of course.'

And she laughed too, and kissed his shoulder, only to yelp in shock as his arms clamped around her and he picked her up.

Her head spun. 'What—'

'Shh.' His mouth stopped any further protest.

Kissing her, he strode across the room, only lifting his head when he came to a door and shouldered his way through it.

Although she'd never felt so small, so light, she protested, 'I'm too heavy—'

'You're tall but you're not heavy. You're like a sapling, slender and graceful.' He stopped and lowered her onto her feet. Hands on her shoulders, he looked into her eyes. 'Or a young goddess, still not entirely sure of her power.'

Enchanted, she felt the rush of delight his words brought push the urgent heat of desire away for a second. Melissa didn't believe them, of course, but she thought she could love him for saying them.

Smiling, she breathed, 'Whereas you are very much aware of yours.'

His mouth hardened. 'I've had ten extra years to learn limits and boundaries.'

She was losing him, she realised with a piercing stab of panic. Quickly, without conscious thought, she reached out and began to unbutton his shirt, fumbling a little until she heard his sharp intake of breath and knew that whatever shadow had darkened his mood had lifted.

Made bolder, she leaned forward, pushing aside the shirt to reveal the smooth swell of muscle in his shoulders. He was big, yet perfectly made, she thought, exulting now. His stillness— the predatory patience of a hunter—encouraged her to kiss his throat, and smooth her hand across that wide expanse of chest.

Sensory overload, she thought dimly, registering the complex textures of sleek skin and crisp hair, his faint personal scent and the sound of her own breathing, sharp and swift, almost keeping pace with the powerful drum of her heartbeat.

In a blurring movement he covered her hand and held it still. 'Take off your shirt,' he said, the words dragging in the salt-scented air.

Melissa couldn't move. After several tension-filled seconds he lifted her chin and gazed directly into her eyes. Time stood still; they exchanged much more than just a look, but her brain was too drugged with perilous excitement to be able to discern what had happened.

'Take it off yourself,' she said hoarsely. She had to swallow a nervous block in her throat to add, 'Fair's fair.'

Hawke's face relaxed. 'Oh, indeed it is,' he purred. 'Lift your arms.'

Poised on a knife-blade of anticipation, she obeyed. He slipped her shirt over her head, but stayed where he was, so close she thought fancifully that she could hear the lazy throb of his heart. Her skin tightened; she didn't dare look up at him in case he was disappointed with her plain bra and broad shoulders.

'Now finish taking off my shirt,' he commanded silkily.

She lifted surprisingly reluctant arms. The fine cotton shirt clung to his shoulders so she had to move closer to manoeuvre the material down. Her throat closed when her breasts brushed his chest, but she persevered grimly until the shirt dropped to the floor.

The sound of the sea in her ears mingled with the rush of her blood and the call of a bird outside.

Hawke said, 'Look at me, Melissa.'

Trembling in a turmoil of emotions and sensation, she lifted her head, and in that charged moment was lost in the wonder of his eyes, narrowed and intent and fierce.

A smile twisted his beautiful mouth, as though for once he wasn't fully in control of himself.

'You are—exquisite,' he said, and slid the straps of her

bra down, unhooking it with a skill she knew she'd anguish over later.

But for the moment anguish had no place in her life; boldly she watched him look at her with darkening eyes and focused attention, noted the subtle hardening of his mouth, the subtle flexing of muscles in his powerful torso.

He took her in his arms; she gave herself to him in a kiss that was at once surrender and demand and acceptance.

She hadn't noticed that they were in a bedroom, but the kiss they shared robbed her of surprise when he pulled back the bed-clothes and lifted her onto the huge bed. Her mind, her eyes, her heart, were too full of Hawke to care where they were.

He came down beside her and began to explore her body with his fingertips, his absorbed focus making her feel as though nothing else mattered in the universe to him but this intense pleasuring. His skilled caresses measured the slender length of her thighs, the narrow indentation of her waist, the soft curve of her breast, and left behind them rivulets of honeyed fire.

Dazed with the molten urgency of her response, she fought back the impulse to pull him on top of her, and smoothed a tentative hand over his shoulder, down the hard, flat six-pack of muscle beneath, following the male wedge to his lean hips and the strong thighs.

'You're beautiful,' she said dreamily, then flushed at the banality of her words.

But his smile wasn't unkind; in fact, it had turned wolf-ish, driven by the passionate instinct to possess. In spite of her vulnerability, Melissa's answering desire banished any apprehension.

As though he'd breached some barrier, he took her mouth in a kiss that ravished the soul from her body, and then kissed a path down her throat, over the warm rise of one breast until he reached the core at the centre.

When his lips closed around it she cried out, a muffled, strangely primal little sound. He began to suckle. Unbearably aroused, her body arched upwards into his in a noiseless plea.

'Not yet,' he said against her skin, his breath hot and tantalising. 'Not yet, princess.'

What followed was a leisurely seduction, a controlled sexual feast that eventually splintered into demand, and then a storm of sensation, so powerful that Melissa gave up thinking and let herself be carried off in the mindless clamour of her responses to Hawke's experienced, tormenting lovemaking.

Lost in the glittering recklessness of his eyes, she followed him into the wilder shores of passion until at last he moved over her, and eased himself into her pleading body, judging it with such fine discrimination that she felt no pain at all.

Oh, the sense of intrusion, of being taken over by something bigger than herself made her catch her breath, but before she had time to think he pressed home, and the pleasure she'd been feeling before rocketed into another plane. Slowly, inevitably, with each thrust of his big body the carnal craving in hers began to build, to dazzle her with even more sensation, to force her up into a dimension she'd never really believed existed.

She gripped his shoulders, fingernails digging into his damp skin, and followed him in a primeval rhythm, taking him, holding him, losing him, only to have him return and begin again.

Consumed by physical euphoria, she arced upwards, taut as a bow, seeking something she didn't recognise, and still he kept up that maddening rhythm until she cried out and clung to him, every muscle tightening around him in a feverish attempt to keep him with her, in her.

His arms bulged with the effort to control his response, but the rhythm quickened; above her, his face hardened into reckless lines and his eyes glittered.

Melissa met his hunger, matched it; the erotic waves surged, coalesced, fought together and finally united in a sweeping surge that hurled her into ecstasy, into such an agony of pleasure that she cried out his name and fell into mindless, helpless rapture.

The same violent fulfilment overtook Hawke; she forced up reluctant eyelids, stunned by the intense power of his release, and watched as he too was thrown into that indescribable region where nothing else mattered.

She knew she would hoard that memory for the rest of her life. Closing her eyes, she let herself soak in the peace of fulfilment, the weight of his body lax on hers, the wonderful wind-down.

When he lifted himself from her, she made a small, inarticulate sound of protest.

'I'm too heavy,' he said, his voice raw.

'No,' she said, glad for once of her height. 'No, you're not.'

He laughed almost silently, but turned to lie on his back. She didn't have time to miss the contact, because one long arm scooped her against his lean body, holding her so that her head lay on his shoulder.

She was glad she had waited, she thought dreamily, even though fear had kept her a virgin so long. Too unsure of her own attraction to risk acceptance for the wrong reasons, she'd preferred to keep herself safe from emotional attachments.

It didn't seem fair that her cowardice had been rewarded with a seduction that was perfect—tender, sensuous, erotic and gentle all at the same time. No wonder Hawke had such a reputation!

Chilled, she tried to empty her mind of everything but the bittersweet present, synchronising her breathing with his, letting herself float on the ebb tide of passion into quiescence.

Neither spoke; Melissa thought that she even slept for a while, and wondered if Hawke did too. She couldn't imagine such a vivid, hard-edged man dozing; he was too aware of his surroundings, too alert, too much a predator.

And was she prey? Or just another notch on his gun?

Stop dramatising, she ordered. This is special for you because it's the first time. But Hawke hadn't even realised that. Perhaps he'd never bedded a virgin before?

She squelched a forbidden pleasure. It didn't matter. It had been a truly wonderful experience for her, but she shouldn't let it assume too much importance, because it wasn't important to him. He might enjoy making love to her, but eventually he'd go back to the loyal, presumably uncomplaining, Jacoba Sinclair.

Eventually she yawned and gave a little wriggle in place of the stretch she really wanted.

He said, 'Uncomfortable?'

'No,' she said quickly.

'I am,' he murmured, and began to stroke her breasts again, his touch sending shivery chills through her. 'Very uncomfortable.'

Surely he couldn't do this so soon? She'd read somewhere that men needed quite a bit of time between bouts of lovemaking—then she looked down the length of their bodies, and realised that whoever had written that had been wrong. Or didn't know Hawke.

'Tell me to stop if you want to,' he said indolently.

His breath in her ear sent signals to her sensitised body, heating that part of her that had only just discovered how acute sexual desire could be. She was suddenly frightened by the realisation that she had no defences against him.

'No,' she said baldly, fighting back an instinctive panic that told her she'd trespassed too far into forbidden territory.

His brows quirked. 'No what?'

'No, don't stop.'

'Good.'

This time it was fast and furious, a white-hot melding of two bodies in such consuming passion that when it was over Melissa could only shake with shock and ecstasy.

Afterwards Hawke brought her fruit and fruit juice and fed her like a baby bird, then slid into bed beside her and held her while she fell into a sleep so profound that she eventually woke completely disoriented.

'What—' she blurted, trying to wrench herself away from the intruder in her bed.

'It's all right.' Hawke's arms were gentle, but he didn't let her go. 'It's all right, Melissa. You're safe.'

By then she'd realised where she was. Colour flooded her skin, bursting up from deep inside her in an embarrassing torrent.

He said on a note of amusement, 'You look like a scarlet poppy. What's the matter?'

'I didn't know where I was,' she mumbled, burying her face in his shoulder so he couldn't read her expression.

'Where you want to be, I hope.' His voice was cool and level and without expression.

'Yes,' she muttered, because she couldn't lie, and why on earth would he believe her if she did?

Some women might be able to fake an orgasm, but Hawke must know that in his arms she lost whatever wits she had and turned into a woman who could only feel.

And, she thought glumly, who really enjoyed what he made her feel.

'So why the pretty blush?'

She lifted her head to peer balefully at him and wailed, 'I don't even know you!'

Hawke shrugged. 'What you see is what you get. I'm healthy, I'm in control of my vices, and there is no one else in my life.'

She had to bite her tongue to stop herself from asking what had happened to the creamy-skinned, red-haired woman he'd been squiring periodically for years. To indicate that she knew about Jacoba Sinclair would tell him that since dancing with him at her cousin's wedding she'd been taking far too much interest in his affairs.

Literally.

'Ditto,' she muttered.

CHAPTER FIVE

MELISSA added sheepishly, 'Although I don't know that I'm actually in control of my vices. It's just that they're not dramatic ones.'

'Tell me about them,' he drawled.

She shook her head. 'No, you'll have to find out about them yourself.'

And wondered with a pang of apprehension if she was taking too much for granted.

'It will be a pleasure,' he murmured, kissing her forehead in an oddly sexless gesture.

Silence ensued. Melissa lay with his arms around her and tried to relax, listening to the sound of the waves on the beach below, the call of a couple of seabirds squabbling over something, the steady thump of Hawke's heartbeat, somehow infinitely soothing.

She felt as she did after hard exercise—pleasantly tired yet stimulated, her body at peace with itself. Unfortunately thoughts scurried around in her mind, worrying at her like evil insects.

'What's the matter?' Hawke asked, his voice remote.

Could he read her mind? She said, 'I should be getting back—I really do need to get some work done.'

The hand in the small of her back held her still while the

other raised her chin so that he could see her face. He said coolly, 'You could work from here.'

Melissa stared at him, her heart leaping like a hooked fish. 'Here?' she said uncertainly, then flushed again.

Stop behaving like a wimp, she commanded, but under his relentless, measuring gaze she felt stripped and exposed.

The corners of his hard, beautiful mouth lifted. 'Here,' he said gravely. 'It has to be more comfortable than the backpackers' lodge and I'd like it if you stayed with me until you have to go. Like you, I have projects, so we can work at the same time.' He paused, and added blandly, 'When we aren't doing other things.'

Melissa teetered on a cliff edge of indecision. Some ancient instinct warned her that if she agreed she'd be giving away much more than a week of her time. He meant for them to be lovers, at least for as long as she stayed here.

Could she do this and then walk away? Or was he suggesting something more permanent than a week spent mainly in bed?

She bit her lip, wishing fervently that she'd had more experience in this man-woman thing. Common sense weighed in to let her know she was playing with fire, but a stronger, more dauntless spirit whispered that if she said no she might regret it for the rest of her life.

He didn't prompt her, gave no indication of irritation or amusement at her hesitation; the green eyes that held her gaze were hooded and unreadable.

'All right,' she said, tossing her cap over the windmill with a vengeance. Then she remembered her manners and said, 'I'd like that.'

He grinned—a wide, buccaneer's smile that sent an erotic little shiver the length of her spine—and pulled her head down and kissed her, an oddly gentle yet utterly purposeful kiss that catapulted her again into the sensual world of his lovemaking.

However, he drew back and got up. 'I think you've had enough for the moment. We'll go down and collect your gear from the backpackers' lodge.'

Melissa turned her flushed face away, because something in his tone told her that he suspected she had been a virgin. Or at least very inexperienced.

Back at the lodge she said, 'Don't come in,' as the car drew up on the forecourt. She felt awkward, aware that the woman who'd left hours ago wasn't the same one who'd come back.

In spite of trying to tell herself that making love to Hawke couldn't fundamentally change her, she suspected that soaring to the heights of ecstasy in his arms had done just that, creating a new version of Melissa Considine.

Or, of course, it needn't have anything to do with the man; she'd been a virgin before, now she wasn't. About time, her friends would say if they knew. No big deal at all.

Except that for her it was.

Hawke scanned her with shrewd eyes, but said, 'All right.'

However, when she appeared in the entranceway he got out of the car and strode towards her, his brows meeting in a frown that made an admiring female backpacker step back in some alarm.

Relieving her of her pack, he said forcefully, 'Don't your brothers feel that you take this impoverished-student thing a bit too far?'

'Sometimes,' she told him. 'But I am a student, and I try hard to be as independent as I can be.'

He gave her a straight look before stowing the pack. 'They're not concerned for your safety?'

She shrugged. 'Occasionally I get threatened with a body-guard, but not here. New Zealand is probably one of the safest countries in the world, and I'm not stupid.'

'Unfortunately we have our share of villains,' he said austerely, opening the passenger door for her. Once inside and behind the wheel, he said, 'I hope you don't hitchhike.'

'I said I wasn't stupid.' Warmed by his concern, she added, 'Of course I don't.'

He nodded and turned the key in the engine. 'There are other dangers.'

'I am aware that some people might hope to influence my brothers through me.' She shrugged. 'Of course, most people don't know that they *are* my brothers, but there's always that possibility.'

He frowned. 'I was thinking of kidnapping.'

'It's not likely to happen here,' she said stubbornly. 'I don't go round wearing a sign that says, "Yes, I'm one of *those* Considines. Prospective kidnappers line up here." Until you arrived at the Shipwreck Bay Lodge no one there made the connection.'

He sent her a narrowed sideways glance. 'Are you sure you're safe with me?'

Melissa said quietly, 'Are you asking me if I trust you?'

A taut silence followed her challenge.

Breaking it, he said, 'Yes, I suppose I am. What do you know about me? I could plan to subject you to unbelievable indecencies.'

'I doubt it.' And she was not going to tell him that she'd probably enjoy—*Where had that thought come from?* Flushed but determined, she finished steadily, 'You have an excellent reputation—hard but honest. And you haven't tried to sweep me off my feet. I've been sure that I could stop you at any time.'

Surprised, she watched a tinge of colour highlight his arrogant cheekbones.

'More sure than I am, then,' he said, negotiating a particularly difficult hairpin corner with skill, not even flinching when a small scarlet sports car hurtled around on the wrong side.

She gasped, but Hawke's hair-trigger reflexes saved them. Judging accurately to within an inch, he steered the four-wheeler almost off the road, taking it through the drifts of gravel with a fine-tuned skill that ignored the cliff only a few inches from the wheels.

When they'd made it around the corner he said through his teeth, 'Spare me from idiots like that, who don't understand the difference between a country road and city streets!' He slung her a glance. 'Do you drive?'

'I,' she said coolly, 'have driven around the Le Mans track.' She grinned and added, 'Very, very slowly. But I'm a good driver. Gabe taught me to drive safely, and Marco taught me how to drive fast.'

As he brought the vehicle to a stop in front of the house he said, 'Your brothers should have told you that there are times when you cannot expect a man to stop.'

It took her a moment to understand that he wasn't referring to driving but to their previous conversation. She said frankly, 'They did, believe me—Gabe used medical terms, whereas Marco was much more earthy. But—if I'd asked you to, you would have, wouldn't you?'

He glanced at her, his mouth a straight line. 'I don't know. I hope so. I'm an ordinary man, princess, not a superhuman. Don't go putting me on a pedestal.'

His honesty pleased her. She said confidently, 'I have two brothers—I know more about men than that!'

And laughed when he laughed, although he said, 'Older brothers tend to be hero-worshipped, I believe.'

'Not since I was ten,' she said pertly.

Inside he said, 'Do you want to share my bedroom?'

Melissa scanned his unrevealing face. Pleased because he gave her the choice, yet unable to discern what he wanted, she said diffidently, 'That's up to you.'

'It's your decision,' he said, sounding a trifle bored.

He'd said nothing about taking their relationship any further, so although she longed to spend the nights with him, she steeled herself to say, 'Then I'll have a separate room.'

Not a sign of disappointment showed in his face. His detached acceptance hurt, but she had to safeguard herself.

'This way,' he said, and after showing her into a glorious room that overlooked the bay and the sea said, 'I'll see you in an hour or so, then.'

Once he'd gone she thought feverishly, I shouldn't be here.

And then, But I want to be.

Even if she came away from this time together with a badly dented heart, she'd be glad she'd decided to stay. Hawke was dangerous, but no one had ever made her feel the way she did when her eyes met his.

Her breath came faster between her parted lips. Or when he touched her...

Put bluntly, she thought, forcing herself to turn and begin unpacking, she wanted Hawke so much she was prepared to risk losing her heart.

Her fingers slowed; she looked unseeingly out of the window. He made love like a god, she thought dreamily...

Five minutes later she shook herself back into life. Scarlet-cheeked and heavy-eyed, she finished unpacking with more speed than care, then took out her laptop and opened it.

After an hour, with the sun sinking lower in the sky and the scent of the sea giving way to the fresh, plum-pudding smell of the bush outside the house, she changed into the crushed velvet trousers she'd worn at Shipwreck Bay. Because it was much warmer here, she topped the trousers with a sleeveless shirt in soft cinnamon. The silk whispered against her sensitised skin, light as cat's-paws across a calm sea.

After an uncertain minute spent hovering inside her room, she plucked up the courage to open the door and come out.

Her heart thumped, because Hawke was two steps away. He looked at her, a light kindling in his eyes, and suddenly her shyness fled and she felt wicked and seductive and more confident than she ever had before.

A reckless smile curved Hawke's mouth, causing the hollow beneath Melissa's ribs to explode into warmth. 'Did you get much done?' he asked.

'Less than I should have,' she admitted, not caring what she was telling him.

His smile turned into laughter, teasing and intimate. 'Me too,' he murmured, and took her hand, lacing the fingers through his. 'My mind was on other things. Let's go and get some dinner.'

Excitement sparked through her, hot and sexy and hungry. 'I should probably tell you that I'm not a good cook,' she said demurely as they walked towards the living-room.

His brows lifted. 'No?'

'No. I wasn't encouraged to go anywhere near the kitchen, and as I like eggs and steak and salads I manage on those.'

He looked at her as though she was something new and intriguing. 'As it happens, I'm not too bad in the kitchen, but the housekeeper has left a meal for us.'

'How long have you owned this house?' The moment she spoke she wished she hadn't, but she wanted to know if he'd been responsible for the spare, practical charm of the place.

He paused, then said, 'I grew up here. My mother was the caretaker most of the time, and the housekeeper when the owner came up for his holidays. When I could afford it I bought the place, demolished the old house and built this one for her.'

A note in his voice told her that there was much more to the story than the bare bones he'd given her. Curiosity poked her with taunting fingers, but she didn't probe any further. 'Does your mother still live here?'

'No,' he said briefly. 'She died several years ago.'

She squeezed his hand, wondering about his father. 'I'm sorry,' she said. 'It's hard losing your mother. I was fourteen when mine died.'

'Not a good time.'

'Is any time a good time?'

Hawke's smile hurt her in some obscure fashion. 'No.' He steered the conversation into less strained channels.

As the afternoon lazed into dusk they sipped the champagne he insisted on opening, and talked the sun down until darkness began to edge over the horizon.

Then Hawke unfolded from his chair and held out a hand to her. 'Come inside, you'll get cold.'

'Not after Shipwreck Bay,' she said wryly, but got up and followed him into the house, charmed by his consideration. 'It's so much warmer up here it hardly seems possible we're in the same small country.'

'New Zealand stretches about a thousand miles from north to south.'

'Someone told me that no place is more than seventy-five miles from the sea.'

'True.'

She nodded. 'No wonder you're such a seafaring nation.'

Innocuous words, said with the casual interest of small conversation, yet beneath them her every sense was alert and on edge, waiting.

The housekeeper *was* an excellent cook, and it was fun to be ordered about by Hawke while they put the finishing touches to the delicious meal.

When they'd eaten they sat over coffee and talked enough to fill several evenings. Hawke had a mind she relished— clever and quick, with flashes of compassion that alleviated his somewhat cynical view of the world. He made her think deeply and intensely and with great exhilaration.

Neither made any open acknowledgement of the reason she was there, but beneath the exploratory direction of their conversation smouldered the heady clamour of sex, sweet and fiery and reckless, heating Melissa's body and preparing her for the longed-for, inevitable end of the evening.

For some obscure reason she both dreaded and desired it, putting off the moment until a yawn took her by surprise.

'Bed,' Hawke said laconically, and got up.

Melissa hesitated a moment, then followed suit.

But he'd noticed; at the door to the room he said evenly, 'Too tired, Melissa?'

His voice caressed her name, and a disturbing, tantalising rush of adrenaline filled her with excited anticipation.

'No,' she returned instantly.

He laughed, and lifted her hand to his mouth, kissing the palm and then the back with as much grace as any elderly French *duc* still harking back to the *ancien régime*.

Melissa shivered, then gasped when he gently bit the fleshy mound beneath her thumb. Sensation arrowed through her, fierce and driven and sharp.

He held her hand to the side of his face, green eyes meeting hers in open, shared desire. He'd shaved, but the erotic friction of his beard sent more little arrows of arousal across her palm.

'Now you know why that particular part of your hand is called the Mount of Venus,' he said.

A dare? Or a taunt? It was hard to tell. But his words made it clear he knew how inexperienced she was.

'Yes,' she said quietly. 'Does it work for you too?'

He held out his hand. 'Try me,' he invited.

The double meaning not lost on her, she took his hand and examined it. Long fingers, strong and straight, and devilishly adept on her skin…

She kissed his palm, then licked the place she'd kissed.

His fingers curled over, as though protecting the place her lips had touched, and his chest lifted and fell. Exhilarated by this addictive foreplay, Melissa waited a few seconds then copied his original caress, letting her teeth sink delicately into the mound beneath his thumb.

His voice was low and dangerous. 'If you want to sleep alone tonight you'd better get the hell behind that door. And lock it!' He produced the last command with the speed and dangerous force of a whiplash.

Melissa looked at him, met his narrowed, metallic gaze and knew an intoxicating surge of power that morphed into a desperate hunger.

'I don't want to,' she said sweetly, and stepped into his arms.

He didn't kiss her; instead he looked into her eyes, his own narrowed and intense. 'You continually surprise me.'

Startled, she returned unevenly, 'I don't know why.'

'Part temptress, part *ingénue*, part minx—a tantalising combination.'

The compliment dazzled her. 'It's not deliberate.'

His smile balanced on the knife edge between challenge and a lazy, almost insolent hunger. 'I know. That's what makes it tantalising,' he said, and closed her mouth with his kisses.

Much later, alone in her bed and running a replay of their lovemaking through her head, Melissa wondered why tears ached behind her eyes. She should be lying stretched out with a smug smile on her lips, purring like a satisfied cat. Hawke had been everything any woman needed in a lover—fierce when she wanted ferocity, tender when she needed tenderness, generous and patient and then wonderfully, excitingly impatient, and in the end he'd been as unable to control his carnal appetite as she had been.

So why the aching, tenuous regret?

Not because he'd left her alone afterwards; she'd made that a certainty by asking for a separate bedroom. And in spite of longing to spend the night with him, she didn't dare. He was too—too much, too overwhelming! So potent was his charisma that she ran the risk of being completely submerged in it.

But she slid into sleep with wet lashes, and when she woke in the morning it was to rain.

'Typical of spring,' Hawke said over breakfast. 'It's usually the wettest season up here.'

The rain poured down onto a sea of pewter silver; beads of moisture collected along the leaves and branches of the trees, and the beach glistened a rich rusty pink.

'It's lovely,' Melissa said. 'I like rain.'

'We should get plenty of work done this morning because it's supposed to ease after lunch. Do you want to do any sightseeing this afternoon?'

She looked at him from beneath her lashes, feeling that intoxicating surge of power when his expression hardened. 'What's the alternative?'

His voice was amused. 'We could stay home, but it seems a shame to miss out on what the north has to offer. And there's always the night.'

'You're sure of that?'

His gaze caressed her. 'Very sure, princess.'

'Then let's not miss out on anything,' she said, wondering if she'd stepped over some unseen boundary.

That day set the pattern; they worked separately during the morning, and in the afternoon he took her around his birth-place. They visited the cradle of European settlement in New Zealand—a small house on a tidal river in Kerikeri, side by side with a neat stone store. Both had been under the protec-tion of a nearby Maori fort.

'Called a pa,' Hawke told her. 'Amazing military architec-ture. See the sides of the hills carved into trenches and pits? Once they held defence walls of timber stakes.'

'That looks old, but the houses seem so new,' she said, smiling. 'Not even two hundred years old.'

'We're a new country. What's the oldest building in Illyria?'

She pondered that. 'Gabe's castle is over six hundred years old, but up the mountain there's a menhir, a huge old stone that was dragged down from the bed of an ancient glacier possibly four thousand years ago and set up to mark the trail and the summer equinox.' The skin tightened across the back of her neck, because like everything else in the country of her ancestors, the menhir had its own legend, one intimately connected to her family, a tale of death and bloodshed and a cruel sprite who protected a fabulous hoard of jewels.

'Quite a difference,' he said, and began to tell her of the culture of New Zealand's original settlers, the people who sailed their huge canoes out of the sunset to fan out across the Pacific and make it theirs.

Melissa was fascinated, but she had to admit that she'd have listened to him even if she hadn't been. It was easy to imagine him as a warrior, bronzed and gleaming as he fought for all that he held dear.

They took the following day off to drive to the northernmost tip of the country—a long, narrow peninsula only a few miles wide, where a white lighthouse looked over the line of colour in the ocean that marked the meeting place of two seas. Hawke showed her the path down the cliff taken by the souls of Maori dead on their way to the afterlife, and the ancient pohutukawa tree that was their last link to the earthly realm.

They ate the delicious seafood of the north, admired huge kauri trees in their remote forest fastness, and one afternoon he took her out to see dolphins and whales and the island called Piercy, a stone archway in the sea.

And every night he took her to a sensuous paradise in his arms.

But afterwards he left her in her lonely bed, where she lay longing for him. He'd said nothing about meeting again after this week was over; this was merely an interlude in both their lives.

'You make me feel old and jaded,' he told her on her last day amidst the remains of a picnic lunch on the beach beneath his house.

She froze for a second. What did he mean?

'I wouldn't exactly call you old or jaded,' she said cheerfully, moving into the dense shade of the swooping, craggy branches of an ancient pohutukawa tree.

Living up to their reputation for inconsistency, the weather gods had turned on a day of high heat and sunshine and soft breezes that flirted across her bare skin.

'Twenty-three is old enough to get married.' Because that was too pointed, she hurried on, 'Old enough to vote, go to war, drive, drink, get into debt and buy a house…'

Everything she said seemed to lead back to settling down!

'Old enough to be considered an adult,' she finished lamely, taking refuge behind an apple. She bit into the crisp flesh and watched him, her heart aching with anticipated pain.

Hawke was lying on his back, clad only in bathing trunks. Water drying on skin burnished bronze by the sun picked out the swell of muscle in thigh and shoulder, the lean strength of his body. Melissa swallowed, prey to a clutch of desire so intense she had to close her eyes against him.

'What's the matter?' he said, his voice lazily concerned.

She shook her head, and he looped an arm around her shoulders and pulled her against him. 'Tell me,' he commanded.

So she did. 'It's been perfect,' she murmured, struggling to produce just the right note of regret and pleasure.

Because the affair didn't mean so much to him. Oh, he liked her, she knew, and he wanted her, but he'd promised nothing, and delivered infinitely more than she'd expected; it wasn't his fault she'd fallen in love with him.

Her heart compressed in her chest, making it difficult to breathe. In love?

Even as the words formed in her brain she rejected them. She did *not* love Hawke Kennedy. He'd shown her that sex could be utterly wonderful, and of course she'd miss him; he was a complex, fascinating man, and behind the formidable, compelling persona he presented to the world was a man of uncompromising integrity.

But she wasn't in love with him.

'Mmm,' he said, and kissed the top of her head. 'Perfect.'

She slipped her arms around him and lifted her face in mute invitation. He kissed her lips, and then other places, and they made love again, protected from any prying eyes at sea by the swooping green umbrella of the tree.

Melissa slept in his arms, but woke to emptiness. She

turned over and lifted herself on one elbow, peering through the silver-backed leaves.

Hawke was standing on the edge of the water. As she watched, storing up memories with a desperation that frightened her, he stooped and picked up something, then hurled it out across the glassy sea with a force that surprised her. The pebble skipped several times before sinking.

She drew a sharp breath and got up, hurrying into her clothes. Tomorrow he'd take her to the local airport at Kerikeri and she'd fly to Auckland and then to Illyria to spend a week with Gabe.

Mordantly she told herself that she had at least twenty-four hours of flying to accept that it was over; until then she'd push it to the back of her mind.

When he returned she was fully dressed and the picnic basket was packed.

Hawke lifted one brow with ironic effect. 'Ready to go?'

Her heart a solid weight in her chest, she smiled. 'Not necessarily. If you want to stay, that's fine.'

'Don't tempt me.' He dropped a swift kiss on her mouth. 'I'm expecting a call, so we'd better head back to the house.'

Melissa looked around and said on a half-sigh, 'I've had such a lovely time. This place is so beautiful—no wonder your parents chose to live here.'

She stopped, a narrowed glance alerting her that she'd touched on a sore point.

'My mother lived here—although not in this particular spot. I grew up in a little old house in the village. My father didn't appear in my life until I was fourteen,' he said curtly. 'He enjoyed a holiday fling with my mother when she was nineteen, but he didn't think to make sure she was all right and she was too proud to contact him when she realised she was pregnant.'

Appalled, Melissa said, 'I'm sorry—I didn't know.'

His broad shoulders lifted in a negligent shrug. 'It's all right—it's common knowledge around here. She contacted him when I started to get into minor trouble. To be fair to him, he accepted responsibility as soon as he found out. He sent me to boarding-school, bought the house and organised a job for her as caretaker and housekeeper.'

He stooped to pick up the basket and set off up the hill. The track up was steep enough to make talking undesirable, which was just as well. Melissa followed him, heart grieving for the boy who'd grown up without a father. Her parents hadn't been happy together, but they had been there…

On the edge of the terrace she turned and looked down at the pink sands of the beach, marked only by their footprints.

Tears blurred her vision. In six hours they'd be washed away by the incoming tide, just as she'd be obliterated from his life.

CHAPTER SIX

LATER, when she could bear to, Melissa wanted to be able to summon every subtle green scent, the tang of the sea, the way the silver backs of the pohutukawa leaves gleamed in the breeze, the gritty purchase of the sand on her skin, the barely discernible song of the tiny wavelets on the beach...

The sights and sounds of happiness, she thought, and chided herself for being sentimental and romantic and stupid.

This was a short affair, a passionate week of lust and intelligent conversation. It meant nothing more to Hawke than that—and she couldn't allow it to mean anything to her, either.

Once inside the house she said, 'I'll unpack the basket.'

'We'll both do it,' he told her.

Then he looked up sharply. 'What—' He pushed Melissa behind him in a gesture as automatic as it was protective.

She froze, because she too heard it—a slight noise that meant someone was walking down the hall.

The door opened and a female voice, slow and sexy and just a little strained, said, 'Darling, thank heavens—'

'Jacoba,' Hawke interrupted, his voice cool and curt. 'What the hell are you doing here?'

White-faced, Melissa swallowed and forced herself to step out from behind him. Jacoba Sinclair, his long-time mistress, stood in the doorway that led to the bedrooms, her famous creamy skin glowing, her hair a fiery wet flood over her shoulders, long legs very much in evidence beneath the short hem of a silken wrap that showed off every slender contour of her body.

Brows rising and a delicious smile fading from her sensuous mouth, she transferred her smoky gaze from Hawke's impassive face to Melissa, who was trying desperately to stay composed while her heart broke into tiny splinters.

'Oh, sorry,' the newcomer said, all expression vanishing from her face. Her long lashes drooped to cover her eyes for a second.

His voice level and ironic, he introduced them, Jacoba as an old friend, and Melissa simply by name—a name that clearly meant something to the other woman. She froze, then gave her head a tiny shake and let her expression relax into a smile that held more than a hint of irony.

'Darling, I know I'm a day or so too early—I didn't realise that you had visitors.'

'Only one,' Hawke said easily, once more fully in control.

'How do you do, Melissa?' The other woman's great grey eyes checked her out.

Awash with chagrin, Melissa felt every grain of sand on her body and in her hair. However, she managed a smile, although it felt stiff on her lips. 'How do you do?' Without looking at Hawke, she said remotely, 'I'm leaving tomorrow, but if it's inconvenient I can go now.'

'Of course you won't,' Hawke said, his eyes never leaving that exquisite face. 'I'll get Mrs Farr to make up a bed for you, Jacoba.'

'Don't be an idiot,' she said with a return of her lovely smile. 'I can do that myself. Which room?'

'I'll show you,' he said.

Struggling out of the frozen wasteland of her thoughts

and emotions, Melissa indicated the picnic basket. 'I'll deal with this.'

Hawke switched an intimidating gaze to her face. 'Thanks.'

She unpacked the basket, concentrating so hard on putting things away that she jumped when the housekeeper arrived and said, 'Let me do that, Ms Considine. You'll be wanting a shower.'

A shower? As she made some innocuous answer and escaped to her room, Melissa thought flatly that a stray thunderbolt would be more appropriate.

She'd believed Hawke when he said that he had no current relationship but Jacoba seemed wholly and thoroughly at home here, and Hawke had obviously been expecting her within the next few days.

And although she'd hidden it well, the other woman had been shocked when she'd heard Melissa's name.

Had Hawke lied?

Sickened, she showered away the salt and the sand and Hawke's touch, scouring her body as though to remove the top layer of skin. Yet even as she did, she knew that, whatever the relationship between him and the gorgeous Jacoba, she'd never be able to chisel him out of her memories.

She grabbed the first clothes her fingers found in the wardrobe, but once she'd got into the jeans and a T-shirt she knew she couldn't let herself be so obvious about her pain. In the end she chose a sleek pair of trousers and a cotton shirt and left it at that, tying her hair back at the base of her neck and using cosmetics carefully to give her pale skin and lips some life.

Then, with her colours nailed to her mast, she went out into the swift northern dusk.

Hawke was waiting for her in the sitting-room, his face remote and controlled. 'I'm sorry about that,' he said without preamble, 'but Jacoba is a very old friend, and she's in a bit of a bind.'

'It's all right,' Melissa responded calmly. She knew just how she was going to play this. She smiled, trying to make it reach her eyes. 'That's what friends are for, after all.'

His eyes narrowed. 'She's eating in her room.'

They spoke of other things, but the connection they'd built had evaporated; it took Melissa all of her energy to keep her end up, and she suspected Hawke wished her anywhere but there.

After a painfully formal meal she said, 'I'd better go and pack. I won't come out again; I can never sleep on planes, so I'll take a mild sedative and hope to get a good night's rest.'

He accepted her decision, although his brows met for a second above his blade of a nose. But outside her door he said in a goaded, furious voice, 'Damn it all to *hell*, princess.'

And he kissed her, using his expertise, his understanding of what excited her to force a response she didn't want to give. Furious with him and herself, she still melted, losing herself for a few mindless seconds in the heat of their passion.

Until he set her away from him and said between his teeth, 'Think of *that* on the plane.'

What sleep her exhausted brain snatched was brief and unsatisfactory, but, though she got up the next morning with dark shadows under her eyes, she held herself together with a strength of character she'd not realised she possessed.

Hawke drove her to the airport; their farewells were studiedly polite and detached, but at the last he said abruptly, 'Ring me when you get home. I'll still be here.'

'Very well.'

With relief so intense it was like the first taste of freedom after long imprisonment, she sank onto her seat on the small commuter aircraft that would drop her off at Auckland within the hour. Staring blindly at the newspaper she'd bought, she willed herself to banish his image from her brain.

The engines roared; once in the air she looked down, and saw a tall figure standing by a four-wheel-drive in the car park. He didn't move and she didn't wave, but she watched him as the plane wheeled, heading out across the brilliant waters of the Bay of Islands and into the real world.

Blinking hard, she opened the newspaper. And there was Jacoba Sinclair, her lovely smile displaying perfect lips and teeth as she walked towards the cameraman. The headline was discreet—NZ Model Returns—but the article beneath implied that Jacoba was on her way to visit her lover, magnate Hawke Kennedy.

Biting her lip, Melissa folded the paper and stuffed it in the seat pocket in front of her, then stared unseeingly out at the green country spread out below.

'All right,' Gabe said evenly, 'I've had enough of your moping. What's your problem?'

Melissa produced a smile. 'No problem,' she returned in a voice that sounded so normal she startled herself.

'You never used to lie,' he observed dispassionately.

Melissa stared down at the small tower that overlooked the swimming pool. Once it had kept doves so that the garrison had fresh meat during the winter; their grandfather had transformed the charming anachronism into a cabaña and party room.

Gabe waited patiently, but his determination to keep digging was palpable. And, being Gabe, he'd worm it out of her.

She said unsteadily, 'OK, so there is a problem, but it's mine, not yours.' And when he stayed silent she continued, 'And I'm long past the stage of running to you, confident that you'll make it better for me. This is something I have to deal with myself.'

He came up behind her and slid an arm across her shoulders, holding her when she instinctively tried to slip free. 'I know the feeling,' he acknowledged wryly. 'Are you all right?'

She kept her gaze resolutely fixed on the orange tiles of the dovecote. The night before she left the Bay of Islands she'd got her period. Oddly enough, she'd wept, but at least she didn't have the possibility of a pregnancy to worry about.

'Lissa?' Gabe prompted, his arm tightening around her shoulders.

The childhood nickname closed her throat. She had to swallow before she could say, 'I'm fine.'

He turned her and searched her face with uncomfortably penetrating eyes. 'You're not in trouble?'

'Not serious trouble,' she said, adding with a smile she tried to make reassuring, 'Just emotional trouble. I'll get over it, Gabe.'

He wasn't satisfied, but after a moment he nodded. 'I suppose it had to happen sooner or later.'

'What?'

'Heartbreak,' he said succinctly. 'If there's anything I can do, tell me.'

In other words he was going to give her the due respect of an adult and let her deal with it on her own. Reassured by his unspoken support, she hugged him fiercely.

She didn't mention his grief over his broken engagement; though she adored him, his shield of self-sufficiency had always prevented her from getting very close to him.

Such heavy responsibility at too early an age, she thought now, and wished he could find the happiness he deserved.

'Do you want to come to Bangkok with me?' he asked, but distantly.

She shook her head and disengaged herself, and this time

he let her go. 'No, I'll stay here, thanks. I've seen too much of the interiors of jets lately.'

'You won't be bored?' He meant, You won't feel abandoned?

'Not a bit. I'll spend the week lounging beside the pool and riding around looking for the perfect place to site a very exclusive lodge.'

The Wolf's Lair, the ancestral castle of the grand dukes of Illyria, guarded a valley of transcendent loveliness, but during the following days Melissa longed for other mountains at the furthermost ends of the earth.

Or a pink cove gleaming beneath a southern sky...

She missed Hawke so much that the depth of her emotions frightened her. If this was lust, she thought, scanning the path up the mountains through her horse's ears, she wasn't ever going to fall in love.

'Ride up to the stone,' the housekeeper at the castle had suggested that morning. 'It's a good place, and it is special for your family. Tell the queen, your ancient grandmother, what is in your heart. She'll help.'

The queen she referred to so reverently figured in tales told by peasants down the generations to explain both the founding of the royal house of Considine and the background of the priceless chain of rubies—the Queen's Blood—that in some symbolic way reinforced their rule. The queen had carried the necklace into war-torn Illyria, only to be slain by brigands at the foot of the great standing stone. She'd been transformed into the deity of the place, guarding her precious hoard until the first Considine had come riding at the head of his band of mercenaries over the pass and down towards the Mediterranean.

To test him she'd manifested herself as an old hag, offering him the rubies and a future in the war-ravaged valley if he'd marry her. A pragmatic man, he'd chosen to wed her, and built the castle.

And to his astonishment, love had worked a miracle, giving the sprite back her youth and her beauty. Together they'd founded a dynasty and since then Considines had kept the valley safe, failing only once—when the dictator had usurped the throne of Illyria.

'I doubt if the queen cares anything about me,' Melissa told the housekeeper.

'She is the mother of your house—of course she cares!' Marya expostulated, thoroughly scandalised. Like every peasant in the valley, she believed implicitly in the old stories. 'Go, it's a lovely day, and you need to ride some of that sadness out of your heart. I'll get a nice lunch for you.'

A fixture at the castle, the elderly woman was a relic of the old days before the regime of the dictator who'd stamped his merciless, murderous brand of repression on the small principality. In fact, she was the only person who'd known where Melissa's grandfather, the then grand duke, had hidden the Queen's Blood; on the death of the usurper Marya had managed to contact Gabe and shown him where to find it.

Melissa obediently accepted the picnic lunch and turned her horse's head towards the ancient route to the pass where a tall glacial boulder marked the boundary of the estate.

She'd always found the place somewhat intimidating; it had an over-abundance of atmosphere. It was too easy to believe that the ancient queen's spirit still brooded at the scene of her murder.

Upended in the middle of a small dell on the mountainside, the stone brooded over a tiny stream that crossed the short grass to run around its granite base, then rippled through trees before throwing itself over the edge of the mountainside into the valley far below.

So peacefully beautiful, it should have eased Melissa's restlessness. After she'd tethered and watered the horse she sat down on the grass, staring at the stone.

Ruggedly ancient, it was marked in a couple of places as though the people who'd dragged it to this place and set it on its end had tried to smooth the craggy sides with their primitive tools. Everything was very quiet; no insect's buzz or trill of birds lightened the heavy silence. Melissa shivered, trying to rid herself of the fanciful notion that the stone was waiting for something to happen—something dreadful...

'They're just old stories made up to explain things,' she said out loud.

Her voice sounded thin and insubstantial. Firmly setting her jaw, she told herself she wasn't superstitious, so it was stupid to let a place get to her.

Marya's suggestion that she tell the spirit of the place what was in her heart made her smile.

But the silence settled oppressively around her; she needed to break it, and talking her misery out loud might help to actually confront her own folly.

So she said prosaically, 'I've fallen in love with a man.'

No, delete that! More strongly, she began again. 'I've had an affair with him.' She wrestled with words, finally saying truthfully, 'I suppose a week is an affair. At least it wasn't just a one-night stand. And he told me there was no one else, but his lover turned up a couple of days too early. She's tall and gorgeous with skin like cream and hair like a dark red waterfall. Obviously I can't compete.'

Although it was autumn the air was too cold, and heavily oppressive. She glanced up over the mountains, but no clouds were forming around the peaks. The sky beamed down blue and bright.

'I thought he was honest,' she said reluctantly. 'As well as sexy and fascinating and clever. But he knew Jacoba was coming—he must have arranged it. It makes me feel like dirt. Especially when I knew that he always goes back to her. I suppose I thought I might be special to him, and it's hurt my pride that I'm not.'

She stopped, listening to—nothing. Yet she felt that her words were still there, formed out of air yet frozen in time.

'Oh, for heaven's sake,' she muttered, scrambling to her feet.

Too hastily, because she stumbled and fell against the stone, only her outstretched palms breaking the impact.

The granite was icy-cold, yet a flash of heat, sharp as an electric shock, bit into each hand and travelled like lightning through her. Gasping, she pulled away, rubbing her hands together as she stared at the stone.

Vaguely above the soft gurgle of the little stream, she heard a distant throbbing—a helicopter, she realised. Gabe, perhaps, although he'd planned to be gone a week, so it might be Marco.

Whatever, she wanted to be away from here, away from the weight of long years burdened by tragedy. Back at the castle in the solid presence of one of her brothers she'd be able to convince herself that the sensation that had torn through her was nothing more than the jolt of cold stone against her skin.

It took her half an hour to ride down the mountain. Still tense, Melissa left the horse at the stables with the groom and walked through the gardens in the shelter of the stone walls.

Inside the castle door, Marya met her, beaming. 'See, I told you she'd help,' she said with satisfaction. 'She's sent you your heart's desire.'

'She's what—?' Incredulity froze her as Hawke strolled out of the great hall and advanced towards her, his hard, handsome face detached and dispassionate.

'Hello, princess,' he said, his tone subtly mocking.

She was not superstitious, Melissa reminded herself, heart picking up speed as an overwhelming delight flamed into life inside her. The fact that the helicopter arrived in the valley at the moment she touched the stone was pure, bewildering co-incidence.

But somewhere she heard the echoes of feminine laughter, softly, affectionately taunting.

Pride stiffened her spine, lent an edge to her words. 'Hello, Hawke. This is a surprise.'

He looked amused. 'Surely not,' he said smoothly.

What the hell did he want? Acutely aware of Marya's interested gaze, Melissa managed to pull herself together enough to say, 'Marya, can you bring some tea, please, to the small parlour?'

It was on the next floor, but the prospect of sharing the confined space of the elevator with him was too intimidating; blindly she veered towards the stairs. 'This way.'

Had he come to claim her?

Get real, she advised herself with cruel pragmatism.

That was the sort of thing romantic men did, and Hawke had told her he wasn't romantic. Sexy as hell, sure, but a man who ran two mistresses didn't have a romantic bone in his body.

Long legs taking the steep flight with ease, he said, 'I noticed signs of activity as we flew over the valley. Gabe has obviously been busy.'

Relieved, she seized on the neutral subject. 'He's determined to provide the peasants here with the amenities the previous ruler withheld from them.'

'Noblesse oblige?'

'Yes,' she said with stiff reserve. 'They suffered badly because they were loyal to our family. It's only fair to repay them for that.'

'I suspected as much,' he said drily.

At the top of the staircase she led the way into the small parlour. 'That's why he agreed to resume the title—because they wanted it. I think he felt some obligation to our father's memory too,' she said, trying to sound normal.

Whatever he was doing here, she had to protect herself. He was addictive; she'd already endured a week of withdrawal symptoms. If she let him get close to her again she'd go through the whole process again, and she wasn't going to allow that to happen.

But oh, her heart soared and she had to stop herself from greedily searching his face, from touching his hand, from letting a smile break through her formal courtesy.

Hawke looked around the room, newly restored to graciousness. Something in his manner made her uneasy.

She hurried into speech again. 'Why are you here?'

'I came to see you,' he said, as though it was the most reasonable thing in the world that he should abandon his lover temporarily to drop in on her.

'How is Ms Sinclair?' she asked with a steely undernote that should have abashed him.

Naturally Marya brought in the tea-tray at that moment. The housekeeper's presence meant that she thought Hawke's arrival too important to be trusted to a mere maid.

Hawke waited until she'd left before answering. 'She's well, and sent you her regards.'

Wordlessly fuming, Melissa applied herself to the courtesies. 'Do take mine back to her,' she said politely, pouring tea with a steady hand.

Hawke accepted his cup and saucer. 'She is not my mistress.'

'Well, of course not,' Melissa said, grimly pleased with her composure. 'Such an outdated word, isn't it? And I'm sure

An Important Message from the Editors

Dear Reader,

Because you've chosen to read one of our fine romance novels, we'd like to say "thank you!" And, as a **special** way to thank you, we've selected <u>two more</u> of the books you love so well **plus** two exciting Mystery Gifts to send you — absolutely <u>FREE</u>!

Please enjoy them with our compliments...

Pam Powers

Peel off seal and place inside...

Lift here

How to validate your Editor's
"Thank You"
FREE GIFTS

1. Peel off gift seal from front cover. Place it in space provided at right. This automatically entitles you to receive 2 FREE BOOKS and 2 FREE mystery gifts.

2. Send back this card and you'll get 2 new Harlequin *Presents®* novels. These books have a cover price of $4.50 or more each in the U.S. and $5.25 or more each in Canada, but they are yours to keep absolutely free.

3. There's no catch. You're under no obligation to buy anything. We charge nothing—ZERO—for your first shipment. And you don't have to make any minimum number of purchases—not even one!

4. The fact is, thousands of readers enjoy receiving their books by mail from The Harlequin Reader Service®. They enjoy the convenience of home delivery...they like getting the best new novels at discount prices BEFORE they're available in stores... and they love their Reader to Reader subscriber newsletter featuring author news, special book offers, book reviews and much more!

5. We hope that after receiving your free books you'll want to remain a subscriber. But the choice is yours— to continue or cancel, any time at all! So why not take us up on our invitation, with no risk of any kind. You'll be glad you did!

GET TWO *Free* MYSTERY GIFTS...

SURPRISE MYSTERY GIFTS COULD BE YOURS **FREE** AS A SPECIAL "THANK YOU" FROM THE EDITORS

The Editor's "Thank You" Free Gifts Include:

- *Two NEW Romance novels!*
- *Two exciting mystery gifts!*

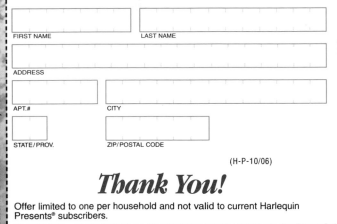

© 2003 HARLEQUIN ENTERPRISES LTD.
® and ™ are trademarks owned and used by the trademark owner and/or its licensee

▼ DETACH AND MAIL CARD TODAY! ▼

Yes! I have placed my
Editor's "Thank You" seal in the
space provided at right. Please
send me 2 free books and
2 free mystery gifts. I
understand I am under no
obligation to purchase any
books, as explained on the
back and on the opposite page.

PLACE
FREE GIFTS
SEAL
HERE

306 HDL EFZ3   **106 HDL EFYS**

FIRST NAME   LAST NAME

ADDRESS

APT.#   CITY

STATE/PROV.   ZIP/POSTAL CODE

(H-P-10/06)

Thank You!

Offer limited to one per household and not valid to current Harlequin
Presents® subscribers.

Your Privacy — Harlequin Books is committed to protecting your privacy. Our Privacy Policy
is available online at www.eharlequin.com or upon request from the Harlequin Reader
Service. From time to time we make our lists of customers available to reputable firms who
may have a product or service of interest to you. If you would prefer for us not to share your
name and address, please check here. ☐

The Harlequin Reader Service® — Here's How It Works:

Accepting your 2 free books and 2 free mystery gifts places you under no obligation to buy anything. You may keep the books and gifts and return the shipping statement marked "cancel." If you do not cancel, about a month later we'll send you 6 additional books and bill you just $3.80 each in the U.S., or $4.47 each in Canada, plus 25¢ shipping & handling per book and applicable taxes if any.* That's the complete price and — compared to cover prices starting from $4.50 each in the U.S. and $5.25 each in Canada — it's quite a bargain! You may cancel at any time, but if you choose to continue, every month we'll send you 6 more books, which you may either purchase at the discount price or return to us and cancel your subscription.

*Terms and prices subject to change without notice. Sales tax applicable in N.Y. Canadian residents will be charged applicable provincial taxes and GST. All orders subject to approval. Credit or debit balances in a customer's account(s) may be offset by any other outstanding balance owed by or to the customer. Please allow 4 to 6 weeks for delivery.

If offer card is missing write to: The Harlequin Reader Service, 3010 Walden Ave., P.O. Box 1867, Buffalo, NY 14240-9952

NO POSTAGE
NECESSARY
IF MAILED
IN THE
UNITED STATES

BUSINESS REPLY MAIL
FIRST-CLASS MAIL   PERMIT NO. 717-003   BUFFALO, NY

POSTAGE WILL BE PAID BY ADDRESSEE

HARLEQUIN READER SERVICE
3010 WALDEN AVE
PO BOX 1867
BUFFALO NY 14240-9952

she's far too successful in her career to need someone to support her financially.'

Hawke's brows rose. 'Neither is she my lover,' he stated uncompromisingly. 'She never has been. She's an old friend.'

An *old*—and very dear—friend who called him darling, and strolled around his house in next to nothing?

Melissa welcomed her anger; it was the only thing that gave her strength enough to say, 'It's not really any of my business.'

'Stop being stupid, Melissa,' he said impatiently. 'Of course it's your business—you and I are lovers.'

'Were,' she said in a rigidly pleasant tone, 'for a few days.'

His hooded, dangerous look sent a chill chasing down her spine. 'I could see what you were thinking, but I couldn't send her away. Things aren't going well in her personal life, so she came to me for refuge.'

Melissa's antennae, always alert for unspoken implications, were on full alert. He was holding something back—perhaps lying. As for his statement that he and the glorious Jacoba weren't lovers—she'd recognised the swift, shocked dismay on the model's lovely face when she'd seen Melissa.

She had looked like a woman who'd been betrayed.

'I hope everything is all right now,' Melissa said smoothly.

Hawke's broad shoulders lifted in a shrug. 'I hope so too.' His tone was level, yet intimidating. 'Do you believe me?'

'Of course.'

And she did; Jacoba's personal life wasn't happy, because the man she loved had just spent a passionate week with another woman. Hawke might consider their relationship an open one, but the beautiful model didn't.

His narrowed, assessing gaze sent prickles of tension through her. She lifted her teacup to her mouth, every nerve stretched on a rack of uncertainty and pain. Why couldn't he be honest with her?

'I don't think you do,' he said curtly, 'although I don't altogether blame you for your suspicion. I know of the gossip that's followed us for years. And I can't prove that we haven't been lovers.' He paused and added with a lethal note in his voice, 'Just as you can't prove that the man who's been escorting you around for the past three months isn't your lover.'

The open attack dismayed her into losing her precarious composure. 'Otto?'

'If you mean Otto Deauville, yes.'

But he must know that she'd been a virgin—well, perhaps not. There had been no obvious signs. She said quickly, 'He's gay.'

'He's bi,' Hawke returned. He watched amazement sharpen her expression. 'So you didn't know.'

'No,' she said quietly. 'And it's none of my business. He's a friend, nothing more.'

His darkly penetrating eyes never left her face. 'I believe you.'

'Thank you,' she said with irony, buying time to think by offering him a plate of an Illyrian delicacy, a sticky plum cake.

The two situations were in no way comparable; Otto was a darling who made no secret of his sexual orientation. Whereas she'd seen Jacoba in Hawke's house, completely at home, and her jealous eyes had noticed the small betraying signs of intimacy, the sort of ease and confidence seen only in people who knew each other so intimately they didn't pretend.

Steeled in her resolve, Melissa asked evenly, 'Why did you come here, Hawke? When we said goodbye both of us knew it was final.'

She held her breath for the answer, appalled by her urgent, desperate desire to hear him say that their week's lovemaking had meant more than just a fling.

He lifted a brow. 'I could see that you thought Jacoba and I were lovers, and I came to tell you that we're not.'

Pride drove her to fake a sophistication she didn't possess. 'I don't know why it's so important to you, but I didn't expect anything more than the week together, if that's what you're—'

'It is not,' he broke in, his voice hard and forceful. 'I miss you, princess. I came to see if you miss me too.'

CHAPTER SEVEN

Joy leaped incandescently inside Melissa. 'Yes, I miss you,' she said unevenly.

Hawke's searching gaze pinned her into her chair. He didn't move, but she saw him relax, as though her words had eased some inner tension.

'I went about things the wrong way,' he said, his voice rueful, and smiled at her.

Melissa's shaky pulse rate soared into the stratosphere. His smile touched something deep inside her, but she wasn't letting him take all the blame. 'We both went too fast.'

'Too greedy—I shouldn't have grabbed at the chance to make you mine. You deserve more than that, and I'm sorry.'

For some reason his apology touched a raw nerve. 'Are you?'

He paused, then said in a goaded voice, 'How the hell can I be sorry when it was so bloody *magnificent*? Just as I knew it would be—in fact, after that first kiss I went back to Auckland to break off a fairly tenuous relationship with a woman there.'

Jealousy gripped her with poisoned talons.

He said, 'We hadn't been lovers, but I felt I owed her some explanation. And although I didn't know whether there was any chance for me with you, I knew I was certainly going to try.'

A fierce delight sharpened Melissa's responses. This, she thought confusedly, was the beginning of a real relationship. The rapturous hours spent in his arms would stay with her for the rest of her life, but at last she accepted that she wanted more from him, an involvement that transcended the physical. And for once, their white-hot need for each other wasn't driving their communication.

Before she had a chance to respond the housekeeper opened the door, a worried frown pleating her sparse brows. 'Telephone for you,' she said to Melissa in Illyrian. 'From His Excellency. He wants you to take it in his study.'

'Very well,' Melissa said, cursing the interruption. Switching to English, she said to Hawke, 'I'm sorry, but Gabe's called on his business line, which means it must be important.'

'Go, take it,' he said, smiling at her with a glint in his eye that lifted her heart as she left the room.

Gabe's study was a charming wood-panelled room he used more as a sitting-room; his real office, the one that hummed with computers and other modern equipment, had been set up off the central courtyard.

Melissa hurried in through the door and picked up the receiver. 'Gabe?' she asked anxiously.

'Sorry, Lissa, but I need a document. Can you unlock the safe?' He gave her the combination.

'Done,' she said after a few seconds. 'What do you need?'

'The folder with "Personal Papers" on it.'

'Got it.'

'OK, my birth certificate.'

Melissa extracted the piece of paper. 'Got it.'

'Good girl.' Someone—a woman—said something at the other end, and Gabe's amusement showed in his voice. 'Lissa, send it to the London office, please. My PA will deal with it.'

'I'll do that now.'

'Thanks. All going well?'

She said, 'Everything's fine.'

But as she put down the receiver and slid the sheet into an envelope she wondered why Gabe needed his birth certificate—and who he had with him. Perhaps someone else was soothing the raw place in his heart that Sara Milton had left behind her...

Too eager to get back to Hawke, she forced herself to write a brief note to go with the certificate and address the envelope before she put both documents inside. She needed a breathing space, because she suspected that Hawke was going to suggest a resumption of their affair, and she had no idea what she'd say to him.

She couldn't bear the sort of relationship he seemed to have with Jacoba Sinclair. Somehow she'd have to make him understand that she wouldn't share—and if he refused to accept that, she'd have to find the strength to send him away.

Marya appeared at the door. 'Is all well?' she asked anxiously.

'Yes, he just needs some documents in London.' Melissa handed her the envelope. 'Can you get this stamped and sent away, please?'

Marya looked down at the envelope with an odd expression, then smiled. 'Of course.'

Mind churning with an alarming mixture of hope and trepidation, Melissa picked up the file to put it away.

A photograph fell out, picture-side up. Stooping, she retrieved it—and staggered, almost falling, when she saw it properly.

Hawke—and Sara, the woman Gabe had planned to marry. Melissa's head swam and she felt sick and cold, yet she couldn't tear her eyes away.

Naked, both of them, Hawke looking at Sara's lovely face

with open desire, and in the background the corner of a four-poster bed with a crimson covering. On the wall behind that was a picture, a nineteenth-century cornfield by an impressionist master

In small white figures at the bottom were printed the time—2:00 a.m.—and the date.

The photograph dropped from her nerveless hand onto the desk. Moving slowly like an old woman, Melissa picked it up and thrust it into her pocket. She swallowed, then put the file into the safe and slammed the weighted door. Nausea hollowed out her stomach; she realised that the odd little whimpering sound she could hear was coming from her throat.

No wonder Gabe had broken his engagement to Sara. How could Hawke have slept with his friend's fiancée?

That was appalling—disgusting—a bitter betrayal of their friendship.

But what hurt her was the realisation that the photograph had been taken at Hawke's château only hours after she had danced with him at Marie-Claire's wedding ball.

'Stupid,' she muttered aloud, clinging to the back of a chair and forcing herself to stand upright. 'You're being stupid.'

That dance meant nothing. She had no right to feel betrayed.

But the wedding had been two weeks after the announcement of Gabe and Sara's betrothal, the engagement that had set every gossip columnist in the world wild with excitement and disbelief. Hawke had been a guest at the wedding, and had offered hospitality to Gabe and Sara. They'd stayed the night before the wedding, but Gabe had had to leave the south of France that night, so Sara had stayed on alone.

Well, not exactly.

Melissa's throat thickened. She wanted to curl up in a corner and howl like an abandoned dog, but forced herself to think. How had Gabe got the photograph? It must have been taken by one of the paparazzi that had dogged the family for the few weeks after Gabe's announcement of his engagement to an unknown interior decorator. Instead of publishing it, he'd sent it to Gabe.

Blackmail?

No. Gabe simply wasn't the sort of man to be blackmailed, and if anyone had wanted to do that then Sara was the logical target—she had much more to lose. But whoever had taken it probably knew enough of Gabe to assume that he'd pay to keep it out of the newspapers.

'Oh, Gabe!' she whispered, aching with pity and pain.

He'd kept his pride, but only his immediate family knew at what cost to himself.

Melissa shook her head, trying to clear it. Wicked Sara—wicked and stupid, because Gabe had truly loved her.

Strangely, when Sara spent the month following the scandalous break-up of her engagement at Hawke's country estate in England, Melissa had thought merely that he'd been chivalrous to a woman with no defence against the baying pack of newsmen who'd trailed her everywhere she went.

Closing her eyes, Melissa thought savagely that she'd been so *naïve*! No doubt he and Sara had laughed at how easily they'd manipulated the situation…

Dragging in a jagged breath, she walked towards the door. Gabe had put an end to his relationship with Sara brutally but cleanly, and she had to do the same—make Hawke realise that there was no place for him in her life, not as a lover, not even as a friend. Loyalty to Gabe—and her own pride—left her with no other recourse.

She stiffened her spine and lifted her head. At heart she was a Considine, she thought defiantly, and she deserved more from a love affair than to come second to Jacoba Sinclair—or third, because Sara might still be in the picture!

She deserved a man she could trust.

So she had to get him out of the castle. Oh, Gabe would find out that the man who'd made love to his fiancée had visited, but she'd be able to assure him that he'd left very soon afterwards.

It took every ounce of resolution she possessed to walk along the corridor, past the painted images of her ancestors in their elaborate clothes and jewels, past the big urn of flowers she'd placed there only yesterday, when she'd thought she couldn't be more unhappy.

Well, she'd been wrong.

Outside the door to the small parlour she stopped and took another shaking breath, praying for courage.

Then she opened the door and walked into the room.

Hawke was standing at one of the windows, looking down at the courtyard below. He swung around and surveyed her.

Eyes narrowing, he demanded sharply, 'What's happened? What's wrong?'

She hated the idea that he knew her well enough to be able to guess that her world had come crashing down on her.

Woodenly she said, 'Nothing—just something that Gabe forgot.'

Her voice sounded flat and tired. He came across the room in a silent rush, and took her cold hands in a comforting grip. Too startled to resist, she was engulfed by his warmth when he pulled her into his arms and held her gently against his big body.

The self-discipline that had kept her upright and functioning deserted her, as though his nearness was a drug so potent it robbed her bones of stuffing and reduced her to limp surrender. Despising herself, she stiffened.

'Tell me,' he said in a deep, calm voice.

She'd rather die!

Thank God for anger; it did what nothing else could do—revived her enough to bring colour to her skin and a sparkle to her eyes, infuse her voice with spirit and pride. 'There's nothing to tell, Hawke. I'm fine, and so is Gabe.'

She pulled back and he let her go, but kept her still with his hands on her shoulders. Whipping up her anger, she met his darkly penetrating eyes, the tension inside her building until she could hardly stop herself from screaming.

'Tell me and I'll fix it for you,' he said ruthlessly. 'Whatever it is.'

If only hysterics were still fashionable—or swooning. She could do with a good faint right now, one that lasted long enough for her to forget she'd ever met him.

White-lipped, she said, 'Nothing's the matter. Let me go, please.'

He did, after he'd steered her to a chair and put her into it. Straightening, he said abruptly, 'You need something—brandy?'

When she shuddered he picked up the silver teapot. 'More tea, then,' he said, and she knew she wasn't going to get rid of him as quickly as she'd planned.

'I don't take sugar,' she said thinly when she saw him add several lumps.

'You need something to counter shock.'

The inflexible tone of his voice told her she had no alternative. Forcing a note of briskness into her tone, she countered, 'I'm not in shock.'

'Could have fooled me, princess.' He handed her the cup and saucer.

She tightened her lips and took it. It was painful to have him minister to her; she lifted the cup, vaguely pleased when her hand stayed steady. She even managed to grimace at the overpowering sweetness of the liquid.

He said brusquely, 'I know it tastes foul but drink the lot. You still look as though you might pass out at any minute.'

'I won't.'

That was better. She sounded more like herself. She just wished he'd sit down; when he loomed over her she felt weak and small and ineffectual.

'Drink,' he ordered.

So she did, listening to the sounds of the valley—the faint hum of a motor at a distance, a bird whistling in the creeper outside, the distant bark of a dog.

And Hawke was right; by the time she'd reached the bottom of the cup the dreadful feeling of inadequacy had faded, leaving her hollow and brittle but more or less in control of herself.

After all, why should she be so appalled? She'd known what he was when she left New Zealand. He wasn't even that unusual; she'd met other men who seemed to believe that women were charming decorations, not real people who could be hurt. They regularly used and discarded lovers, often keeping up the façade of a marriage that suited them. Her brothers were different—but perhaps not, she thought bleakly.

Perhaps she thought they were different because she loved them. Perhaps they too sought nothing more than recreation from their lovers...

'I'd like to know what's going on in your head,' Hawke said unexpectedly, startling her into looking up at him.

He noted the faint patches of colour above her sweeping Slavic cheekbones, and allowed himself to relax a little. She was recovering.

'I'm just thinking this tea is horrible,' she said politely, her cool tone and dismissive.

What the hell had happened? She'd been in command of herself before that phone call. Oh, she hadn't believed him when he'd told her he and Jacoba were only friends, but something had happened while she'd been taking Gabe's call that had shattered her completely, draining the colour from her skin and deadening her topaz eyes.

The intense protectiveness of his response startled him. He wanted to pick her up and keep her safe, make sure that nothing like that ever happened again.

Now she lifted her head and met his gaze squarely. She was, Hawke realised, angry—no, make that furious, and it was with him.

What the hell had her brother told her?

Subtlety wasn't the way to deal with this—she'd just hide behind that patrician air of breeding and ignore any hints. So he'd use the sledgehammer approach.

'What did Gabe say to you that shocked you so much?'

Her direct gaze didn't waver, but a challenge flamed in the depths of her eyes and her mouth hardened.

'Nothing. I'm sorry I drooped on you—I had a bad night last night, and I must be more tired than I thought, but I'm fine now.' An ironic smile ghosted across her full, passionate mouth. 'Mind you, I'll probably be on a sugar high for the rest of the day.'

Damn it, she was hiding behind her armour of politeness. Hawke fought back the temptation to smash through it. He didn't even dare touch her, because any attempt at shaking the truth out of her would soon be overcome by their powerful mutual need.

Whatever else had changed, that hadn't, he thought with savage satisfaction. For a few seconds she'd rested in his arms so sweetly, as though he was all she craved, and when he'd inhaled the soft fragrance that was hers alone he'd felt his body clamp with an urgent hunger that was dangerously more than desire.

He was getting in too deep. The week they'd spent together had only honed his hunger for her, not sated it.

And then it struck him; there could be another reason for the faint. Without any pretence at finesse, he demanded, 'Are you pregnant?'

He lunged for her as the colour started to drain again from Melissa's face. But she didn't crumple; she seemed to reach deep inside herself for the strength to put out a hand and fend him off.

After long seconds, she said harshly, 'No. No, I'm not.'

She's lying, he thought, and an incredible, bewildering joy filled him. 'You weren't taking a contraceptive.'

Heat flamed into her pale, exquisite skin, before fading as swiftly as it had come. 'We used protection. Anyway, it wasn't the right time.'

'You know perfectly well that there is no such thing as a safe time. And condoms have been known to fail.'

'Not this time,' she flashed back.

Bluntly, allowing a note of intimidation into his voice, he said, 'Melissa, if you are pregnant, or if you could be, tell me now.'

She stood up, very gracious, very much in control of herself, the princess on her home ground. 'I am not pregnant.' Another touch of colour highlighted her cheekbones but her voice was perfectly steady—steady and cool and precise—as she went on, 'I've had physical evidence that I'm not. Thank you for coming to see me, but it really wasn't necessary. We both knew that the week we spent together was just a pleasant interlude.'

His eyes narrowed. *'Pleasant?'* he said menacingly, furious with himself for letting her matter-of-fact comment sting. It had to be his pride, but he was an adult, beyond that sort of macho, high-school swaggering. 'That's a put-down for something that I, for one, enjoyed enormously. You must be an excellent actress, because from your reaction I assumed you did too.'

Melissa flushed again, but held his gaze without flinching, her eyes cold and clear and determined in her white, composed face. 'I did. But it happened—where did you call it?—*two stops past the ends of the earth*. It was an erotic fantasy. This is real life, Hawke. I can't believe you expected it to last—such episodes never do.'

'For all your charming pretence of innocence, I assume this isn't the first time you've indulged in such an—*episode*.' He knew he was being petty; some distant part of his brain was urging caution, wondering if the reason he was so angry was because for once he was the one being rejected.

Blank-faced, she shrugged and glanced away. 'My past is none of your business, just as yours is nothing to do with me. Accept it, Hawke—it's over.' She paused, and when he didn't answer went on steadily, 'I assume you're on your way to the capital for Alex's big round of meetings?'

'I do have business with the prince,' he said, making up his mind, 'but not immediately. I'd hoped to talk to Gabe while I was here.'

'Gabe won't be back for a week.'

She looked back at him, her mouth so firmly compressed it was impossible to believe she'd once kissed him lovingly all over, her lips hot and testing against his skin, her hair a honey-warm flood of silk that tantalised every cell on his body.

Which responded with brutal efficiency to the memory. Something flamed in the tawny-gold eyes. He saw the effort it took her to dampen it down, and some ruthless inner part of him rejoiced.

She was lying. He knew it as clearly as if she'd spelled it out. Either she knew she was pregnant, or suspected she might be. And although she'd tried hard, she hadn't convinced him that she was indifferent to him.

In a husky voice she said, 'Normally I'd ask you to stay, but I'm leaving tomorrow myself.'

Quick recovery, he thought, admiration warring with frustration. He wanted to kiss her into submission, feel her yield as she'd done so many times in his arms, but although she might surrender, it would change nothing.

Frustrated by her intransigence, he said, 'In that case, of course I'll leave.'

Melissa should have been relieved.

Of course, she *was* relieved. But she felt Hawke's words like a blow to the heart.

Before she could come up with a banal, polite response, he said, 'Have you anyone to look after you in case you have another attack of faintness?'

'Of course there are doctors in the valley now,' she said, forcing her voice into its crispest mode. 'And it won't happen again.'

Because the cause of her temporary weakness was standing right there in front of her, straight brows knotted in a frown and arrogant jaw jutting as he surveyed her blank face.

Once he left the castle she'd feel better. Her nerves were stretched too far, sabotaged by a longing for him to go that battled her yearning for him to stay. More than anything in the world, she wanted him to convince her that everything would be all right, that he'd never slept with Sara. Or Jacoba Sinclair.

Or the pretty actress Lucy St James, who'd been wretched enough to attempt suicide when he'd dumped her.

But that sort of thing only happened in fairy tales. Nothing could alter the photograph, just as nothing could alter the fact that Melissa had gone against every warning, every instinct, and let herself be seduced by him.

Worse than that, she'd actively encouraged his seduction. He'd given her every opportunity to retreat, and she'd ignored each one.

What did that make her? A fool. She said, 'I'll tell Gabe you called.'

'Thank you.'

Chilled by his tone, she gestured towards the door. 'I'll come down with you.'

'Don't bother,' he said with cool insolence. 'Shall I send your maid to you?'

'No, thank you. I'm fine,' she said with a flash of irritation. At least he'd accepted her assertion that she wasn't pregnant.

And then she saw their son—a small boy with his father's strong bone structure and long limbs, pedalling a scarlet tricycle down a long gravelled drive, countenance alive with glee as he laughed up at them both...

Stunned, she blinked, and the brilliant little image winked out as though it had never been.

Hawke's voice broke through her stunned astonishment as he grabbed her and held her upright. 'What the hell—!'

He shook her slightly, then when she stared at him in disarray he picked her up and carried her across to a large, comfortable sofa and sat down with her in his arms.

'That's it,' he said, his voice cold and uncompromising. 'I'm not going until you've seen a doctor.'

'I'm not sick.' Mad, perhaps, but not sick.

'*Something's* wrong with you.' A ruthless finger tipped her chin so he could inspect her face.

Melissa closed her eyes to shut him out, but she couldn't

ignore the other sensory signals assailing her body—his faint, evocative scent, the warmth of his body, the strength of the muscles that flexed against her when he moved.

Grittily she said, 'Let me go, Hawke. I'm perfectly all right.'

His voice deepened into intimidation. 'You have two choices. Either your housekeeper puts you to bed, or I do.'

Melissa's lashes flew up and she met a gaze of such formidable purpose that she blinked.

'Make up your mind,' Hawke said.

'I won't be told what to do in my own house!'

'Castle. And you'll not only be told, you'll damned well do it,' he said in a flinty tone, and with her still in his arms stood up, a display of such raw strength that she gasped.

'Oh, all right!' Melissa knew when she was beaten. If she didn't let Marya put her to bed he'd have no compunction about doing it himself. And she didn't trust herself within ten metres of a bedroom with Hawke.

She added stubbornly, 'Now put me down. You'll look silly wandering around the corridors searching for my room.'

He grinned, and dropped a swift kiss on her mouth. 'Why would I do that?' he drawled, setting her down on her feet, although he kept an arm locked around her shoulders. 'I'd ring for the maid and tell her to take me there.'

'She wouldn't do it.' But she suspected that Marya would take one look at his indomitable face with its strikingly sculpted features and do whatever Hawke told her to.

'Want to bet?' He pulled the bell rope left over from the days of Melissa's grandparents.

Marya must have been hovering because she appeared instantly at the door, black eyes snapping with interest when she took in Hawke's arm around Melissa's shoulders.

Not, Melissa thought, that she looked surprised. Sometimes she wondered whether Marya was entirely of this world; there was something ageless and antique about her.

Without raising his voice Hawke spoke slowly and clearly in English. 'The princess is ill,' he said. 'She needs to rest.'

Marya bobbed a curtsey to him and turned to Melissa. 'Can you walk?' she asked in Illyrian.

'Of course I can,' Melissa said, desperate to get away from this strength-sapping closeness.

But she wasn't given the chance. Again Hawke swung her up into his arms. Marya gave a quick, hidden smile that to Melissa's shocked eyes smacked of satisfaction, and led him out of the room, escorting him without compunction to the elevator that took them up to her tower room.

Once there he set her on her feet, and examined her face and then the room. 'Charming,' he observed coolly. 'Did you design it?'

'No,' she said, prickling with resentment.

Marya interposed in her fractured English, 'His Excellency do it for Princess Melissa's birthday.'

He said, 'Whoever did it knew you, obviously. It fits you.'

Melissa, who adored the room but privately thought it too romantic for her prosaic soul, said tartly, 'Far from it. He got a decorator in from London.'

She managed to force herself to look straight at Hawke. Even as she chose the dismissive words she had to say, her pathetic brain was memorising everything about him, from the exact shade of green in his eyes—dark now, and deeply shadowed like the huge chunk of precious greenstone in the lobby at Shipwreck Bay—to the sensuous twist of his hard, beautiful mouth.

Some complicated knot in her stomach began to unravel. She knew what she had to say—why were the words so difficult to summon? Dry-mouthed, every sense quivering and alert, she said, 'Thank you. I'm sorry it's been so unproductive a visit. I'll tell Gabe you wanted to see him.'

'Don't worry,' he said aloofly. 'We'll get together some time when it's convenient for both of us.'

He nodded to her and swung on his heel. Marya started after him, but he told her abruptly, 'Take care of your mistress. I can find my own way out.'

'Go with him,' Melissa said harshly in Illyrian as he left the room. 'He'll get lost.'

Marya smiled broadly, but followed him, leaving Melissa to stand in her gracious room and listen for the sound of the helicopter taking him out of her life forever.

CHAPTER EIGHT

AT THE sound of the chopper engines, Melissa let herself relax, not even trying to mop up the painful tears.

From behind Marya said in Illyrian, 'He will come back.'

'Not Hawke,' Melissa told her wearily. 'Not this time.'

The housekeeper came round to stand in front of her. 'Why did you send him away?'

Melissa blew her nose and straightened her shoulders, re-pressing an inner shudder at the memory of that damning photograph. She felt sick and tainted, as though the unknown photographer had smirched all her dreams.

Which was ridiculous, because it was Hawke and Sara who'd done that. 'He's not trustworthy—neither honest nor honourable,' she said curtly.

Marya scanned her face. 'But you love him.'

'I *want* him,' Melissa corrected. 'I'll get over it. Don't tell Gabe.'

The older woman looked offended. 'That he came?'

'I'll tell him that.'

'But not that you love this man and sent him away?'

Without correcting her again, Melissa nodded. Let her think it was a love affair gone wrong, instead of a week of passion that had now turned into a sordid fling.

The housekeeper said, 'I will not tell your brother that because it is not his business.'

With a wry smile Melissa said, 'You know Gabe, he'd make it his business.' And he'd already suffered enough at Hawke's hands.

The older woman said thoughtfully, 'They are strong men, your brothers and this man.'

Too strong for her, Melissa thought with a shiver, wondering if Gabe's strength had ever been used against a woman. He'd always been a refuge to her, her adored protector, yet she sensed that he could hurt as well as shield.

At least he didn't have the character flaw that marred Hawke, she thought, swallowing back the threatening tears. Apart from his ill-judged engagement to Sara, Gabe had never been caught up in any scandal. He'd had affairs, but he seemed to have the knack of staying friends with his lovers; certainly none had spilled their anguish to the tabloids.

The photograph of Sara in Hawke's arms was burned into her retinas; when she closed her eyes she could see it so plainly she feared she'd never get rid of it.

Marya said, 'So be careful. Mr Kennedy is accustomed to getting his own way, and I do not think he surrenders to any opposition.'

A chill raced the length of Melissa's spine. She said firmly, 'He won't be a problem.'

After all, he'd never said anything about loving her; his heart was probably armoured against such a bourgeois emotion. Lust was entirely different.

And if she'd read him wrong, pride would stop him from coming again when she'd so definitely turned him down. He could have any woman on earth—beautiful women, women of sophistication and wealth and intelligence. Why would he bother with her?

Unless her surrender satisfied some sick desire in him to sleep with the woman of a man he saw as an enemy? But why? Had Gabe beaten him in some business battle?

'I will bring you a warm drink,' the housekeeper said firmly. 'Sit down and compose yourself.'

'Thank you—I'd like that.'

Alone again, Melissa listened to the rising pitch of the helicopter rotors.

Had their affair been a matter of revenge? Had Gabe bested Hawke in a business deal—and was Hawke the sort of man who'd callously use an enemy's woman to exact some sort of retribution?

'No,' she said aloud, sickened at the thought.

But he'd slept with Sara only weeks after she'd become engaged to Gabe. And if Melissa hadn't been Gabe's sister, would he have followed her to the Bay of Islands?

Probably not. Her heart clenched in pain as the helicopter's engines roared, gathering strength for lift-off.

From the narrow window, an arrow slit in the walls of the tower room, she watched the chopper fly up against the bulk of the mountains into the blue, blue sky, taking all joy, all comfort and delight with it.

Turning away, she muttered, 'Good riddance. And you are *not*—not now, not ever—in love with him.'

Love needed time to grow, to mature, to forge links between two people—time they hadn't had. OK, so during that idyllic week together they'd spent hours talking, exploring each other's minds and values, but both, she knew now, had been holding back.

She'd sensed that it would be dangerous to reveal too much

of herself to him. Instinct had warned her to protect herself, but in spite of that she'd let the feverish, consuming attraction between them convince her that he was a man of honour and integrity.

More fool her. Recognising this ache in her heart as cheap longing for sex would banish it more quickly, surely?

That night she stayed up late, pretending to read while she resisted the sleazy urge to go and check the photograph again for signs of tampering. It lay like a wicked secret, hidden in the drawer of her dresser.

She should put it back into Gabe's files, but it was like armour, the only way she could stave off a weak yearning to forgive Hawke.

Her eyes hadn't played tricks on her; the two lovers were Hawke and Sara. As for being computer-enhanced—that was just wishful thinking. After all, it had convinced Gabe, who'd have had experts check it. If she needed further proof, it was provided by the fact that Sara had stayed with Hawke after the break-up of her doomed engagement.

'Which just goes to show how green you were,' Melissa told herself, crawling into bed.

Green as grass, more naïve than a schoolgirl—and stupid with it!

Now she was going to have to learn to live with her folly.

She woke the next morning with a headache, and reluctantly agreed to breakfast in bed, more because she knew Marya would worry than because she felt bad.

After she'd crunched the toast and drunk two cups of coffee, Marya appeared at the door. 'You are feeling better?'

'I will once I've had some fresh air,' Melissa said, making up her mind. 'I'm going riding.'

'A good idea,' the housekeeper approved.

It took a while, but before she'd left the fertile fields of the valley for the mountain track the throbbing had eased. Not so the pain in her heart, however often she tried telling herself it was nothing more drastic than wounded pride.

The clamour of distant church bells reminded her it was Sunday; she stopped the mare and listened, the joyous tolling intensifying the emptiness in her heart until she saw the golden valley beneath her through a haze of tears.

Blinking ferociously, she focused on the castle, four-square and defiant on its craggy height above the rich land. The last scarlet leaves of the vine that shrouded the stone walls had turned into brown wraiths and fluttered to the ground. Soon it would be winter; snow would blanket the fields, and the skies would burn so brightly blue they'd make her eyes water. Before long drifts would close the pass in the mountains that led to the rest of Europe, letting the valley ease back into a serene time of preparation for the following spring.

At least no one had to fear starvation now. Singled out for punishment because of their fierce loyalty to the prince and their grand duke, the people been denied even the most basic aid. Now they knew that Alex, Gabe and Marco would make sure no one went hungry.

And they had the equipment to produce more food from the fields, a hospital to take care of illness, and better roads.

This was her future, not grieving like some Victorian virgin over a cad who'd seduced and betrayed her. She had a job to do here, a debt to repay to these people whose loyalty had cost them so much.

Tourism would inevitably change their lives; she hoped for the better, by providing jobs and skills and options they'd never had. But with increasing sophistication they'd lose something too.

Hoping they'd think the gains worth the losses, Melissa gave a light tug on the rein. She would not let her stupidity rule her life. OK, so she'd had a wild affair with a man who turned out to be not worth it; she'd get over it.

She had to get over it.

'Come on, girl, what's the matter?' she asked, leaning forward to pat the sleek chestnut neck. The mare fidgeted and tossed her head, then took a couple of steps up the trail towards the menhir.

'Well, all right,' Melissa agreed with a tight little smile, letting her mount have her head. 'It's not as though I've got anything more interesting to do than wrap up the project on marketing New Zealand's luxury lodges.'

The church bells fell silent as they climbed and the prevailing hush collected around them like a cloak. Melissa set her teeth. She wouldn't give in to this irrational fear.

Perhaps loving Hawke had given her a taste for danger, she thought with a bleak smile.

But of course there was no danger. Many times she'd heard her father describe the sense of isolation on the trail, telling her it was because their ancestor, the queen, guarded the ancient path, still watching in spirit over her valley and her descendants.

Perhaps he'd been right. Marya obviously thought so.

'So if you brought him here,' she said aloud, not hiding the flippancy of her words, 'perhaps you could now show me how to get over the man! I don't think I'm made for languishing and moping and wishing things were different.'

Incredibly she held her breath, but of course nothing happened—no flash of lightning, no vision like the little image of Hawke's son that she'd seen yesterday.

Hawke's, perhaps, never hers. Yet her hand moved to touch her waist protectively, and for a few defiant seconds she mourned a child who'd never be conceived.

This maudlin repining certainly wasn't going to help her get over Hawke!

The mare flicked her ears back, and went steadily on, climbing as though she had a purpose in mind. Which she had—the spring in the grassy glade where the menhir kept its ancient surveillance.

Once watered and allowed to crop some of the grass, the mare stood patiently when Melissa tethered her to a convenient branch.

This time she made sure she didn't touch the menhir, but Hawke's words about the weight of history rang in her ears. Who had dragged it down from the heights all those thousands of years ago? What arcane ceremonies had been performed around its base?

And why—more recently, but still long, long ago—had a queen come adventuring over the pass with a treasure in rubies, only to meet her death right here?

Melissa had hoped for peace. Instead she felt a wild anticipation, a kind of subliminal thunder in her blood, as though she faced the biggest challenge of her life.

Her senses sprang into full alert; hardly breathing, she listened with ears preternaturally honed for a sound—any sound—to break the heavy silence. Tension clutched her by the throat; she thought she could taste it, feel its pressure on her skin.

Slowly she turned, and there he stood beside her mount, one hand on its neck—watching her.

Hawke.

Panic kicked her in the stomach with such force that she couldn't speak. Not a muscle moved in the compelling, forceful face; his gaze stayed fixed on her, and she knew that if she obeyed her rioting instincts and ran he'd catch her before she'd taken more than a few steps.

He came towards her. 'Princess.'

He spoke gravely, without inflection or nuance, and she whispered, 'What are you doing here?'

'Waiting for you.'

Melissa's heart stopped, then raced into action as adrenaline poured into her bloodstream. He meant it; she could see the ruthless resolve in his expression, hear the ruthless authority in his tone.

Jumbled responses banished rational thought and common sense, urging her simultaneously to run and to talk reasonably to him.

In the end she said, 'Why?'

Stopping too close in front of her, he lifted a satiric eyebrow. 'Because I don't trust you to tell me the truth. I'm going to take you to France so I can find out for sure whether you're pregnant.'

Hugely relieved, she took refuge in anger. 'I told you I'd had a period!'

'Difficult to prove,' he said inexorably. 'When's your next one?'

'In three weeks' time,' she said automatically, before foolishly letting pain and hurt pride override common sense. Flinging the words at him like sharp stones, she said, 'I don't have to prove anything to you. And even if I didn't know for certain that I'm not pregnant, what does it matter?'

He looked at her with something so close to contempt she took a step backwards. The charged stone of the menhir against her back iced through her, shocking her into a sudden gasp before she jerked free.

Hawke grabbed her. She thought for a moment that he was going to shake her, but his fingers relaxed and he set her free. 'It matters,' he said between his teeth. 'If it's my child you're carrying, I want some say in its future.'

She said unevenly, 'I am not—repeat n-o-t—pregnant.'

'Then why are you so fragile?'

Melissa stared into eyes as green as glacial ice, frozen and fierce like those of some great bird of prey. Not for anything was she going to tell him how the menhir affected her. He'd think she was mad.

Though at the moment that might not be such a bad thing. She said furiously, 'I am not! You gave me a hell of a fright—appearing like some blasted demon out of the forest!'

Then, scared because his proximity was working its usual magic on her heightened senses, stirring them into heated, carnal awareness, she blurted, 'Hawke, listen to me—why would I lie to you?'

'Because you're aware that your pregnancy is something I feel intimately involved in,' he said, lashes drooping to hide his eyes.

She looked past him and cried out.

'What the hell…!' In one explosive, flowing movement he whipped around.

'My horse!' she said into his back. 'She's gone.'

His taut muscles relaxed. He turned and took her elbow in a grip of steel. 'She's already on her way home.'

'You untied her?'

'Yes.'

'She could end up anywhere!' Without success Melissa tried to yank her elbow away, but he urged her towards the trees. Towed across the short grass in his merciless grip, she protested hotly, 'Not all animals find their way home.'

'This one will.'

'How do you know?'

He glanced down at her and seemed to make up his mind. 'Will it make you feel better if I fly over the track so that you can see for yourself?'

'Fly?' she parroted.

'I don't plan to force you to walk over the mountain,' he said impatiently. 'The helicopter's just through the trees here.'

She dug her heels in. 'Hawke, this is crazy! I'll never forgive you, and if that doesn't scare you enough, neither Gabe nor Marco will forgive you either.' Her eyes searched his uncompromising features but she could see no sign of reaction. Heart sinking, she finished desperately, 'If I am pregnant I'll tell you.'

'I don't trust you,' he said coolly.

And that was that. He didn't trust her, so he'd decided to abduct her. 'You are an arrogant bastard,' she ground out.

An ironic smile touched his hard mouth. 'Just as arrogant as you are, princess.'

Baffled, she glowered at him. He was a bewildering mixture of contradictions, and she didn't know how to deal with him. She should be scared, but she sensed instinctively that he didn't mean her any harm.

And while her mind was telling her that his behaviour was beyond outrageous, it was impossible to surrender to righteous indignation when her every cell was acutely responsive to his lean, dangerous attraction, the smooth strength and dynamic grace of his body.

She said coldly, 'I don't know what you hope to gain by this.'

He shrugged and urged her through the trees to another clearing, where a helicopter waited silently. Melissa looked about for the pilot, but there was no one else there.

'Are you flying the chopper?' she asked.

Hawke's straight black brows rose. 'I do my own dirty work.'

It seemed oddly principled behaviour for someone who clearly thought nothing of abduction. She said staunchly, 'When I don't come back Marya will contact Gabe.'

'She knows where you are. She packed for you.'

'*What?*' Marya had done that? Why?

He answered her unspoken question. 'She seemed to think it was a good idea.'

'And I suppose she told you I was coming up here.'

He nodded.

Melissa said angrily, 'She must have gone mad!'

'She seemed a very astute woman to me.'

At least someone knew where she was. And Gabe would be back in a week; once he got to Wolf's Lair he'd bring her home.

The thought should have cheered her up. It didn't.

But she refused to be hauled off to Hawke's château in the south of France—the very place he'd seduced Sara.

Melissa saw her chance when he let her go to slide open the chopper door. She waited until he had his back to her, then swung around and raced away into the trees, long legs covering the ground as she dodged between clutching obstructive branches, hoping desperately that the gloom of the forest would swallow her up.

His yell sounded far too close; heart hammering, she sped up, forcing her legs to go faster. Ahead, she saw a lightening of the shade as the trees thinned out. Too late, she remembered the cliff face, and the waterfall dashing itself onto rocks at the base...

Strong arms lassoed her and brought her to the ground. By some miracle Hawke managed to land under her, rolling onto his back to take the full effects of the fall himself, but she lay gasping and winded across him.

Her own pulse roaring in her ears, she listened to the rapid thunder of his heart against her cheek. His arms were so tight around her she could barely breathe, and although she knew he was furious with her she had never felt safer.

He said between his teeth, 'You stupid little idiot! What the hell did you think you were doing? There's a cliff about twenty metres ahead.'

She swallowed and said thinly, 'I didn't—at least, I did know it was there. I just forgot.'

He swore under his breath and sat up, supporting her. The bones of his face stood out in stark prominence and his eyes were molten in his oddly pale face. 'Did I frighten you that much?'

'No,' she shouted, fighting back a humiliating desire to burst into tears. 'Of course you didn't. I'm angry—you have no right to fly in and drag me off like some blasted lord of the manor just to reassure yourself that I'm not pregnant!'

Her mouth dried as something altered in his gaze, flickered in the brilliant green depths, then flamed into fire.

Thoughts dissolved and disappeared. 'No right,' she repeated vaguely, every cell in her body acutely aware of a delicious languor robbing her of coherence, drugging her into sexual surrender.

'Damn.' Eyes locked on to hers, he shook his head as though to clear it. 'I didn't intend...'

She swayed against him, and the powerful muscles in his body contracted. Then he groaned, and his head came down and he kissed her, his mouth hot and seeking and completely determined.

Relief and anger fuelled hungry, unsparing desire. Melissa went up like skyrockets beneath him, kissing him back with such fervour she thought she might burn to a crisp in the embers.

Hawke's seeking lips travelled the length of her throat;

against the frantic pulse at the base he said with raw intensity, 'Tell me to stop.'

Dazzled by the tumultuous sensations clamouring through her, she gasped, 'Stop.'

But she might as well have been begging. It didn't help when she summoned the energy to whisper, 'Please...'

Her tone betrayed her, turning the word into a plea for more. He lifted his head and looked at her, his gaze, she thought victoriously, a claim and a demand and an understanding that the last thing she wanted was for him to stop.

'Please kiss you?' His voice deepened into a sensuous purr. 'Please make love to you?'

Dumbly she nodded, because if he didn't love her now she'd die of frustration.

Deftly Hawke opened the lapels of her shirt and whipped it off her, leaving her clad only in her bra. She shuddered, her fingers busy with his buttons, and kissed the brown neck she revealed, then bit, her teeth sharp against his skin, her tongue following the delicate line of indentations she made.

His big body went rigid; he said something beneath his breath as she savoured the fresh male taste. Then his mouth found the peak of her breast beneath the soft material of her bra, and he suckled strongly.

Pleasure, sharp and keen as pain, tore through her. Gasping, she clung to him and arced into the heat and power of his body.

Melissa longed for the ecstatic release she knew he'd give her, and, although her brain made a final feeble protest, her body took over. She slid her hands beneath the open front of his shirt, her palms slipping across corded muscles, and pulled his lean hips into intimate contact with hers. Shivers of carnal delight racked her at the thrusting pressure against the most exquisitely sensitive part of her anatomy.

Always before there had been a gentleness she'd wanted to believe was tenderness—a long, tantalising build-up of arousal. That didn't happen this time; in the aftermath of danger they behaved like savages, tearing at clothing in their desperation to free themselves until finally they came together in reckless passion.

Yet even in their feral hunger, Hawke didn't use his great strength against her. She found that she could meet and match him, her body twisting and turning against his, her arms holding him so close that each breath, each heartbeat, each shudder of sensation became mutual.

Almost immediately Melissa arched, her incoherent cry taking her by surprise when rapture swamped her in spreading waves of erotic fulfilment, tossing her higher and ever higher until she groaned in pleading, wordless fulfilment.

Hawke followed her into that ecstatic place, joined her there, and then came down with her, down and down into the sweet lethargy of release as the sweat dried on their skin and the sound of the little waterfall echoed mockingly in their ears.

At last she said dreamily, 'I'm sorry.' And shivered.

He knew what she was apologising for.

'Hell,' he said into her hair, 'so am I. I didn't dare call out in case it spurred you on to run faster. Why aren't you representing Illyria at the Olympics?'

His arms tightened around her, but only for a second. Levering himself away, he rolled over onto the bed of their clothes and stared up into the dark branches of the tree above them. 'And now we've made love without any protection at all.'

Melissa's gaze followed a small brown bird with a scarlet collar. It perched on a branch and peered down at them as though it knew exactly what had happened. At that precise moment she didn't care about the lack of protection; her body was too satisfied, too lax with passionate pleasure.

'It's the wrong time of the month.'

'Perhaps. However, that settles it,' he said evenly, turning his head to look at her with cool, remote eyes.

A chill settled in the region of her heart. 'Settles what?'

'You're coming to France with me, and you're staying until we know for sure.'

She said with quiet conviction, 'Hawke, believe me, if I'm pregnant, I'll let you know. There's no need for this.'

'Get dressed,' he said dispassionately.

CHAPTER NINE

MELISSA had to say it. 'There's the morning-after pill.'

Tension filled the silence that followed, until Hawke responded in a voice totally without expression, 'Is that what you want?'

'No,' she said without thought. 'I'm sorry, but it's just not…not…'

Her voice trailed away. She closed her eyes, shutting out the brown bird with its bright throat, wishing she too was totally driven by instinct, every decision made by the need to survive.

But she wasn't; she had to live with the results of her actions, and she'd been foolishly irresponsible.

Nevertheless, she couldn't bear the thought of rejecting a child. Eventually she finished lamely, 'I wouldn't.'

'Then it's not an issue,' he said with aloof courtesy. He sat up and reached for his shirt. 'Let's go. And if you try to run again I'll tie you up.'

'I haven't got the strength,' she said, then ducked her head to hide her scarlet cheeks and shocked eyes.

'Lassitude is another indication of pregnancy, I believe,' he said levelly.

'I am *not* pregnant,' she ground out.

'Are you on the Pill?' At the swift shake of her head, he

said austerely, 'Then quite possibly you are as of a few minutes ago. Get dressed, or I'll do it for you.'

Sapped of will, she surrendered, hastily fumbling her way into her clothes as the distance between them grew to unbridgeable lengths.

They were near the helicopter when she asked, 'What do you plan to do if I am—if there is a problem?'

'We'll deal with that if it eventuates.' His tone was detached. 'But it's only fair to tell you now that I have no intention of being an absentee father. If it's at all possible, children should live with both parents.'

And Melissa understood at last why he was doing this. Not for her—probably not even for a possible child—but to appease the little boy who'd grown up in the Bay of Islands waiting for the father who'd finally appeared too late. 'I see,' she said quietly, her heart gently, noiselessly, breaking.

Until then she'd hoped—without even realising it—that he'd been unable to live without her, that somewhere beneath the glorious glitter and fire of passion was some sort of solid bedrock, the sort that might be a basis for love.

Instead, he was merely making sure that no child of his would be left like him, longing for a father.

She understood his need to take responsibility for any child of his, but couldn't he see the contradiction? His mother had been abandoned after a brief affair, yet Hawke didn't seem to care about the hearts he'd broken.

Nevertheless, that image of a bright, lonely little boy stopped her from any further protest. Soon—within a few days—she'd be able to prove to him that she wasn't pregnant. All she had to do was stick out those days.

Hawke flew the helicopter with the skill and confidence of long experience, taking the machine out over the cliff so that the valley spread like a picture in a book of fairy tales beneath them.

A moment later he touched her arm and indicated the mare, ambling towards the castle. One of the grooms had come out of the stables, and as they watched the chestnut's pace quickened.

'Amazing how much power sugar lumps have over horses.' Even through the earphones Hawke's dry tone made Melissa smile as the helicopter swooped around and began to climb up and over the mountain.

Just over the border they transferred to a small private jet—flown by a professional pilot, Melissa noted wryly as she wondered why on earth she wasn't kicking and screaming and demanding that he contact the police.

Mainly because he was clearly Hawke's man, but was it also because she hoped in her innermost heart that somehow she'd be able to make a dent in Hawke's formidable reserve?

Perhaps. But the photograph she'd found in Gabe's files nagged at her, hurting her with its open eroticism. She would not allow herself to love a man who'd slept with her brother's fiancée.

Yet she'd just had wild sex with him, and nothing had ever felt so good.

OK, so analyse, she thought stringently, aware that she was clutching at straws. Was it because he was her first lover, so she had nothing to compare it to?

Possibly, although listening to her friends' initiation tales had prepared her for the aftermath of the first time to be a mixture of acute self-consciousness and pain, to be followed by the wistful question, *Is that what all the fuss is about?*

Her mouth relaxed into a small, subtly sensuous smile, instantly wiped, because of course it was Hawke's skill—some of it gained with Sara—that had made him the perfect first lover.

The thought of him and Gabe's fiancée together filled her with nausea, yet she had to admit that Hawke made her feel cherished and feminine and exciting. And he'd taken her to heights she'd only ever read about.

Judging by her friends' experiences, that was a rare thing.

Skin tightening, she wondered if that was why she found him so irresistible—because for the first time in her life she felt like a passionate woman.

As the plane droned on she stared at the changing landscape beneath, trying to sort her muddled thoughts.

'What are you thinking?' he asked, disturbing her.

She looked up and found him examining her face with half-closed eyes. 'Nothing,' she said automatically.

'I hope you're not preparing any more bids for freedom.' Although his tone was even and without inflection, she heard the warning in the words.

Mutinously she shrugged.

His brows lifted. 'You won't get the chance.'

Melissa turned her head and stared blindly down at the dun-coloured Alpes Maritimes beneath, and the bright blue Mediterranean. '*I* hope you don't plan to keep me prisoner.'

Reflected in the window, Hawke subjected her to a narrow, cynical smile. 'Indeed I do,' he said with silky emphasis. 'You're going to spend the next week so close to me that nothing will separate us. You'll eat with me, swim with me, sail with me, ride with me and sleep in my bed with me until you can show me that you're definitely not pregnant.'

Fierce rejection warred with white-hot temptation. It would be torture of the most exquisite kind—forced into such perilous, erotic intimacy with him, all the while knowing that he'd been Sara's lover, and that because of that nothing could come of it.

Melissa swallowed to ease her dry throat and said thinly, 'I'd rather you locked me in the dungeons.'

'That sort of thing went out with the French Revolution,' he drawled. 'I'm not some mediaeval despot.'

'If you insist on such close contact,' she argued, 'you'll be making it more likely that I'll end up pregnant.' Colour touched her skin, and she turned her head away to resolutely stare at the landscape beneath.

He was silent for so long that she thought he'd decided to ignore her. Finally, he admitted, 'You are, of course, perfectly right. Very well—you'll sleep alone.'

She bit her lip. 'Why won't you believe me?'

'Princess, you're not stupid, so don't pretend you are. In New Zealand you were the epitome of good health, so your interesting pallor at the castle alerted me that something had happened.' He paused, then added caustically, 'And even if you weren't pregnant with my child before, my lack of control on the mountainside just increased the chances dramatically.'

Melissa kept her face turned to the window so he couldn't see the shock in her face. The note of contempt in his voice knotted her stomach.

Unexpectedly, his voice so formal it iced through to her bones, he added, 'Some instincts are beyond reason, I've discovered. I'm sorry.'

'You weren't *entirely* responsible,' she said stiffly, hating him. In a similar situation, would he have made love to any woman?

Probably. She had to keep telling herself she didn't really know him; the man who'd dazzled her in New Zealand wasn't the real Hawke Kennedy. The real Hawke Kennedy was a serial philanderer.

Whatever, there could be no future for them. Apart from

Gabe's furious disappointment if he ever found out about their intemperate, reckless affair, there was the fact that for her, faithfulness was essential in any relationship. However much she loved Hawke, she could never marry him if he didn't share that belief. She'd experienced first-hand the strain her mother's love affairs had wreaked on her parents' marriage.

And after seeing that photograph, how could she ever trust him?

Better a clean cut now, she thought miserably, than the kind of misery her father had endured—that Jacoba Sinclair was still enduring.

But first she had to get through unbearable days of closeness to Hawke until she could prove she wasn't carrying his child under her heart. No doubt she'd be able to get a pregnancy test as soon as they arrived at his château—and nowadays, she dimly recalled, they were so accurate they could tell within a few days of conception.

Then she'd leave, and go back to her real life. OK, so it stretched ahead of her in a grey, dreary expanse of formless days, but she'd enjoyed it before; she'd learn to enjoy it again. These past weeks had been an aberration, a highly coloured fairy tale of epic proportions, driven by lust and drama and her own overwhelming emotions.

Surely one day she'd be able to see Hawke's photograph in the newspaper without feeling this wild, heady clamour of desire.

The plane landed at Cannes Airport; Hawke was clearly a celebrity here. She wasn't surprised when he produced her passport with his own.

Hawke spoke excellent French, surprising her. Like her brothers, Melissa was fluent in three languages—English, French and Illyrian; she could also make herself understood in Spanish and was reasonably adept in German. But she'd expected Hawke to be the same as many English-speakers, unable to converse in any language but his own.

Well, she'd been wrong in that, as in so much else about him.

Outside in the warm southern sun they were met by a large, sleek limousine. Melissa hadn't been to Hawke's château before, though she'd seen photographs of it—a restored sixteenth-century pile of honey-coloured stone amongst palm-studded gardens bright with flowers.

But now, as they drove up to it, she realised that photographs had entirely failed to convey what it was really like. The mellow stone walls might dream beside the blue Mediterranean, but it had been built with much more than sunshine and holidays in mind. Planned for defence, in its day it had repelled raiders and enemies.

Just like the Wolf's Lair.

'Do you live here?' she asked politely, startled by how little she knew about him.

'For three months of the year, yes. But I'm a New Zealander; I spend as much time at home as I can.'

The car slid between impressive open gates flanked by stone towers. Although there were no obvious security personnel around, she knew their arrival would have been watched and checked, and stifled a pang of regret for the freedom of her stay in New Zealand.

As they walked up the steps to a massive front door, Hawke said coolly, 'Welcome.'

She opened her mouth to answer, only to close it again when the door swung open and a large man moved majestically towards them, his dress and air indicating that he was the butler.

Hawke's hand tightened on her elbow, and together they walked into the cool luxury of the château, scented with flowers, the original utilitarian starkness of the building long

hidden by panelling and parquet floors, chandeliers and mag-
nificently moulded ceilings. Melissa eyed the monumental
marble staircase sweeping up from the entrance hall.

So this was where Sara had stayed—with Gabe the night
before Marie-Claire's marriage, and with Hawke the night after.

Keeping her eyes away from the man beside her, Melissa
wished with bitter intensity that she'd known about the photograph before she'd agreed to spend that week in Hawke's
beach house. If she had, she'd have left the Bay of Islands the
day he'd arrived there, and none of this would have happened.
Eventually she'd have forgotten that she went up in flames
when his cynical, amoral mouth took hers.

Some treacherous part of her murmured, But you'd never
have known that in his arms you know the true meaning of
rapture...

The butler mentioned respectfully that there were urgent
messages for his master.

Hawke frowned, then turned to Melissa, cool green eyes
raking her face. 'I won't be long. Your room is waiting—perhaps you'd like a rest.'

Woodenly she said, 'Thank you.'

Hawke's eyes narrowed, but he nodded and strode off.

She directed a smile at the butler, who murmured, 'This
way, Your Highness.'

Your Highness! She'd assumed that no one besides the
Illyrians would be interested in her new status; it seemed
she'd been wrong again. Straightening her shoulders, she
went with him up the splendid eighteenth-century staircase.

The bedroom was huge, and superbly decorated in a skilful
combination of comfortable modern pieces and priceless
antiques. Melissa looked around, then stopped abruptly, cold
nausea driving the colour from her skin.

On the wall opposite the window was a picture, a glorious. misty painting by one of the impressionist masters, its mélange of colours assembling into a cornfield. She recognised it instantly, and didn't need the crimson covering on the bed to tell her that this was the room Sara had slept in. The cornfield painting had been in the background of the photograph.

Outraged despair iced through her. Was this the room Hawke reserved for his mistresses? Had Jacoba slept here too?

It took Melissa all of her energy not to spin on her heel and rush out; only the thought of trying to explain her horror to the butler stopped her.

Think! she adjured herself. Making time, she strolled across to the window and looked out. Relief surged through her as she took in the view of the mountains.

Turning, she said sweetly, 'Oh, what a pity. The mountains are glorious, of course, but I'd rather hoped to be able to see the sea.'

The butler's eyes widened, but only for a second. 'Certainly,' he said in a wooden voice. 'If Your Highness will just wait here for a moment or two, I'll send for tea and have another room prepared.'

She was sipping tea with desperate eagerness when Hawke came in. He looked at her with cool dispassion. 'I'm sorry the room doesn't suit you,' he said evenly.

She set down her cup and saucer, almost wincing when they clattered against the polished top of the table. 'I just mentioned that I'd have liked a view of the sea,' she said, her polite tone matching his.

'I thought the mountains might have reminded you of home.'

She kept her expression under strict control. 'If it's inconvenient, then of course—'

'It's not inconvenient,' he said tersely.

Relief flooded her, although she was tempted to confront him, tell him that she knew about him and Sara, heap her scorn and contempt on him.

But loyalty to Gabe forbade that. She said starkly, 'I don't react well to threats.'

One black brow shot up. 'Threats?'

Colour skimmed her cheekbones. 'You threatened me with imprisonment.'

Hawke stopped himself from clenching his hands into fists. He suspected she was deliberately provoking him—punishment for those maddened minutes spent in his arms in Illyria?

Well, she couldn't despise him any more than he despised himself. Growing up with a father whose intelligence almost matched his lack of discipline had given Hawke a hearty contempt for anyone unable to control themselves, yet Princess Melissa Considine, delicious irritant, shattered his self-control every time she looked through her lashes at him.

Or smiled. Or walked, with that seductive sway of her hips. Or said anything in that clear voice that turned husky and eager when she was aroused…

He'd give anything to be able to undo their impassioned lovemaking; in fact, the one thing that muted his cold self-contempt was the knowledge that she'd been equally desperate and hungry.

Even now, with the prospect of pregnancy only too likely, he could feel the sensual tension of attraction smouldering between them. His muscles contracted; he had to stop himself from striding across and hauling her out of that chair to wipe the serene confidence off her face with a savage kiss.

He wanted her witless with desire, her eyes huge and sleepy beneath heavy lids as she looked at him, her mouth ardent and sensuous against his skin…

He said bluntly, 'I've ordered a pregnancy test.'

The colour in her face ebbed away, but she nodded regally. 'Thank you.'

The butler appeared in the doorway. '*Madame*'s room is ready,' he said after a glance at his employer.

Melissa got up, carefully avoiding Hawke's gaze. 'Thank you,' she said, smiling at the butler, who bowed and left after a dismissive nod from his master.

'I'll take you there,' Hawke said with freezing restraint.

The new room was in the old part of the château. Mindful of her excuse for changing, Melissa went across to the window and gazed at the broad expanse of the sea beneath.

'Thank you,' she said steadily. 'It's lovely.'

A humourless smile curved her host's mouth. 'I'm glad you like it,' he returned, equalling her smooth formality. He glanced at the slim watch on his wrist. 'I have some work that won't wait, unfortunately, but I'll collect you in an hour's time and we can walk in the gardens. If you want to shower, the bathroom is through that door there. A maid will unpack.'

The thinly disguised orders set her seething with resentment. 'Thank you,' she said, showing her teeth in a smile that held no humour.

The small bathroom off her bedroom was opulently lined with marble in mellow, sensuous shades of pale rose and cream. Melissa sighed with relief beneath the pounding spray, letting her muscles relax from the tension that had gripped them since she'd turned in the glade and seen Hawke waiting in the shadows like some vengeful god from a dark, magnificent underworld. She spent a long time in the shower, scouring herself until she felt free from his touch, his possession, his complete domination of her emotions and senses.

Back in her bedroom, her suitcase had disappeared. She

opened the door of a superb armoire and surveyed the clothes Marya had packed for her. Everything she might need for a week's stay, she realised, including her handbag. She reached into her bag to see if she had money. Flinching, she felt her fingertips skim a glossy surface—the photograph, she thought sickly.

Well, it was just as well. The next time Hawke touched her she'd recall that, and the remorseless tide of desire would ebb into disgust.

She chose a pair of white trousers, topping them with a rich nutmeg-coloured voile shirt, its loose fit, mandarin neckline and elbow-length sleeves more concealing than anything else she owned. Sandals the same warm colour finished off the outfit; she regarded herself in the mirror and decided that no one could accuse her of dressing to seduce.

Here on the Mediterranean it was warmer and more sultry than the crisp air of the valley, so after she'd reduced her hair to order with the drier she left it to fall loosely around her shoulders.

Turning away from the mirror, she stood undecided. Her gaze ranged along the curved wall of the big room, its ancient stones almost covered by a splendid tapestry of lovers and goddesses. This room was furnished in a more solid, antique way than the bedroom she'd rejected. It reminded her of the castle in Illyria.

After eyeing the magnificent bed against the side wall, Melissa frowned as her gaze traced the outline of a door in the panelling.

A dressing-room?

It didn't seem likely; the armoire was big enough to hold an entire wardrobe of clothes.

Feeling oddly like Bluebeard's wife, she walked across and

tried the handle. When it turned under her fingers she let out a slow breath and eased the door open.

It led into another bedroom. Melissa's breath caught in her throat. Poised for flight, she frowned as she examined the bed, a twin to the one in her room, and the curved stone of the facing wall. Her heart rate picked up; she stepped back and hastily dragged at the door.

Only to freeze when Hawke strolled into her line of sight, a towel knotted around his lean hips, the faint sheen of moisture on his broad shoulders proclaiming that he too had been showering.

Melissa must have made some startled involuntary movement because he whipped around and saw her framed in the doorway. His expression clamped into formidable austerity, then relaxed.

'Come in if you want to,' he said, and dropped the towel with casual insolence.

Her heart jumped; always before she'd been so dazed by lust that she'd never really appreciated the loose-limbed litheness of his splendid physique. His bronzed, sleek strength overwhelmed her; she felt her mouth dry out and had to avert her eyes before she was able to demand hoarsely, 'What are you doing here?'

'You wanted to change rooms, so naturally Jacques assumed you'd prefer to be closer to me.' His voice deepened into laconic amusement. 'He probably thinks he's assisted your secret fantasies.'

Stupid! Oh, she'd been so stupid! 'You could have told me you'd be right next door!'

'Why?'

Ears honed to every small sound detected the rustle of clothing. Obstinately resisting the temptation to sneak a look, Melissa kept her eyes fixed onto the tapestry on the wall.

He finished, 'Yours is the only other suitable room with a sea view. I believe it's called being hoist with your own petard. You can stop so defiantly admiring the tapestry now, I'm decent.'

From now on she'd have, superimposed on her inner eyelids, an image of Hawke walking into sight like some pagan, powerful god, the sort of Mediterranean deity who seduced any woman who took his fancy. Heat bloomed inside her in response, fierce and every bit as pagan.

Feeling unutterably idiotic, she let her eyes drift cautiously sideways. He had pulled on a pair of jeans and was getting into a T-shirt, shrugging the fine material over the smoothly flexing muscles of his shoulders and torso.

Melissa jerked her gaze away, her mouth so dry she could barely articulate, but it was far too dangerous to let that image linger in her mind. 'What *is* a petard?'

'An ancient weapon,' he told her, irony tempering his words. 'The builders of your Wolf's Lair and this place would have known all about them. A metal cone was filled with explosives, hoisted to wherever the walls needed to be breached, and exploded. To be hoist with one's own petard was to meet a violent death from one's own weapon. Now it means to suffer the unwelcome consequences of one's own actions.'

'I see.' She took a couple of calming breaths and blurted, 'I hope this door has a lock.'

His flat, lethal gaze reminded her that those ancient gods of the Inland Sea were capable of killing with a glare.

'No,' he said, a note of contempt in his voice setting her teeth on edge, 'but I can promise you I won't be opening it from my side.'

'Good.'

She stepped back, but as she went to close the door behind her he said in a tone made hurtful by a cutting note of sarcasm, 'Of course, if you feel you want to open it, you'll always be welcome.'

His words sent a shiver of excitement down her spine, but she knew better than to answer. She didn't even slam the heavy wooden door, although she made sure it was firmly shut.

Biting her lip, she tried a few more deep breaths. Although they hadn't soothed her nerves much by the time Hawke knocked on the door to the corridor, she did feel marginally more in control.

However, his coolly dispassionate examination shattered the small progress she'd achieved. 'I like your hair like that. Why do you pull it back so severely?'

'It gets in my eyes,' she said with prim precision, joining him. As he closed the door behind them she said, 'I should probably have it cut.'

'I don't think so.'

She'd kept it long because her mother had once said a little irritably, 'No, Melissa! Short hair would make your head look too small. Tall girls like you need balance.'

It was, she thought, her one asset, although she'd have liked it to be a more dramatic colour than a soft golden brown.

She glanced at Hawke's blue-black head, and wondered why it was intensely sexy for a man to be tall and wide-shouldered and long-legged, whereas it was completely the other way for women—except, she reminded herself scathingly, for gorgeous models who managed to look willowy rather than lanky!

And if she kept reacting to every tiny nuance of expression in his tone, in his face, she'd go mad. The only way to get through this with any degree of dignity was to pretend she was on an ordinary visit to an ordinary château in the course of her ordinary life.

So she'd make ordinary social conversation while walking down this superb staircase. 'You once said that New Zealand will always be your home, so why did you buy this place?'

OK, so it sounded laborious and banal, but that was infinitely better than revealing that her whole body sang because he was walking beside her.

'I liked the idea of owning a castle by the sea,' he returned easily. He slanted her a glance that told her he knew exactly what she was doing, his mouth curving into an enigmatic smile. 'Besides, it was just about to fall down. Perhaps because I come from a country with—at the most—a thousand years of history I hated to see it collapse into ruins.'

'It looks wonderful now.' She avoided his too-knowing scrutiny by gazing around as they walked through a side door into a courtyard.

They strolled on, Hawke making the trials of restoring a heap of ancient stone both amusing and fascinating.

Rounding a corner, Melissa breathed, 'Oh!' And on a gurgle of laughter, 'It's outrageous, but it looks wonderful!'

A plastered wall, painted a burgundy colour that only the sea could compete with, had been further enlivened by a vine, its deep pink flowers an astonishing yet highly successful contrast to the colour behind. Small purple flowers blazed regally at the base, separating the wall from the stone pavement. A shaded nook held pots of pink geraniums, their round green leaves contrasting with some bronze-leafed herb.

Melissa's eyes found another corner where a slender stem held aloft several large tufts of strappy bronze leaves. 'Didn't I see something like that growing in New Zealand—in meadows and beside streams? Only they were bigger and green.'

'Yes, it's a cabbage tree. Not that we have meadows in

New Zealand, and the only fields are playing fields. We have paddocks.'

Her heart somersaulted at his smile. Dazed, she had to look away and swallow, trying to rein in her unruly thoughts enough to make some sort of sensible response.

She managed it, but not before the silence had stretched a little too long. 'So you planted a cabbage tree to remind you of home. And I was sure you didn't have a sentimental bone in your body!'

'Ah, you can take a New Zealander out of the country, but you can't take New Zealand out of the New Zealander. I also have a pohutukawa growing on a terrace overlooking the sea. Can you still remember how to say it?'

And in spite of everything, her spirits lifted. 'Of course I can.'

CHAPTER TEN

MELISSA half-closed her eyes to concentrate on repeating the name of the plant, carefully imitating the way Hawke had slid the liquid syllables together.

The pause that followed brought her lashes up, her heart leaping when she saw that he was watching her with an odd expression.

Almost, she thought wonderingly, as though he'd been powerfully affected by something.

But in a level, almost sardonic voice he said, 'That was brilliant. Have you been practising?'

'No,' she said, shaking her head. 'But if you can learn to speak excellent French, I can make an effort to pronounce a Maori word correctly.'

'I didn't actually learn French as such—my babysitter was an elderly Frenchwoman who'd spent her life travelling the Pacific in a yacht with her husband. When they got too old for the life they came ashore to the Bay of Islands. She looked after me while my mother worked and because she and her husband spoke French together I grew up bilingual.' He paused, then said in an edged tone that forbade any further discussion, 'I owe them a lot more than a good French accent. He was the only father I had.'

He took her arm and turned her towards a doorway in the wall. 'Come and say hello to the pohutukawa.'

Had this been why he'd offered Sara refuge on his estate—a sense of responsibility, the need to make sure she wasn't pregnant with his child?

He might have no morals when it came to sex, Melissa thought with compassion, but deep inside the high-handed man was iron-clad self-sufficiency that hid a small boy who'd spent all his formative years missing a father.

The arch led to another terrace, this one paved in mellow old bricks; low plants edged the rocky cliff that fell into the sea. Tucked against the château wall, a pergola covered with a green vine sheltered a big shady area, set with loungers and tables and chairs.

The pohutukawa stood to one side, its silver-based leaves causing her a pang of homesickness.

In a voice she struggled to keep steady, she said, 'It looks very happy here. But then why wouldn't it? It's a beautiful setting.'

'As beautiful as the beach house?'

A note in his voice sent a sharp little shiver the length of her spine. But of course he wasn't thinking about that perfect week—or regretting its abrupt conclusion.

'Differently beautiful,' she said, forcing herself to sound brisk and assured. 'Just as the Bay of Islands is different from Shipwreck Bay, although both are transcendentally lovely.'

'I'm thinking of selling this place.'

'Why?'

He shrugged again and looked around him, his brows drawn together. Tall and bronzed in the warm sun, he looked supremely sure of himself. Bleakly, wistfully, Melissa envied him that unspoken inner confidence in his ability to deal with anything that came his way.

'I don't need it. More and more of my business is based in Asia and North America, and if I need to spend time in Europe I have a house in London that's perfectly adequate. Besides, I want to live in my part of the world. I've already sold the country house in England.'

Chilled, she wondered if perhaps he felt some regret about his affair with Sara, if selling the English estate and now the château was his way of washing his hands of the past.

Shame? She glanced across at his profile, steel-cut in the gentle Mediterranean sun. No, she thought savagely, it was impossible to imagine him feeling that.

Ignoring the familiar twinge of pain, she said crisply, 'It makes sense, I suppose.' And, not giving him time to answer, she changed the subject with a total lack of finesse to ask about the plants.

Surprisingly, he seemed quite knowledgeable about them. When she commented on this he said coolly, 'My mother was an ardent gardener. I must have learned from her without realising it.'

Melissa gave in to her secret craving to know more about him. 'The plants here look very similar to the ones in the garden at your house in the Bay of Islands.'

'It's a bach,' he said, and smiled at her enquiring lift of the brows. 'South Islanders call them cribs, but in the north any holiday house is a bach. As for the similar vegetation—yes, it gets hotter here in summer, but the climate is fairly similar if you ignore the cyclones that occasionally hit the north of New Zealand.'

When she didn't answer, he glanced down at her and frowned. 'Come and sit down. There's an excellent view over the bay from here.'

He steered her towards a seat in the shaded arbour. An old

rose bush, still covered with flowers, diffused a rich, exotic perfume into the salty air. Melissa smiled when a petal floated down to land on her face, and lifted her hand to flick it away.

Her fingers collided with Hawke's; eyes holding her gaze, he removed the petal, but his fingers returned to her skin, stroking delicately. Tiny, sensuous rills of pleasure flowed through her, alerting every cell in her body.

Abruptly he straightened and turned away, his expression aloof. 'What my father didn't tell my mother when they had their affair was that he was married—to a woman with enough money to keep him in the style to which he'd become accustomed. I think he loved my mother, but he was too lazy, too dependent on his wife's money, to make the break.'

Melissa had to stifle a cold anger. Perhaps his father didn't want to. Had Hawke inherited his cavalier attitude to women from his father?

No, she thought, watching his face. He might have come to feel some affection for his father, but he clearly despised him too. So why did he follow in his footsteps?

The thought niggled as she said tentatively, 'If your memories of the place aren't happy, I'm surprised you keep it.'

'His wife never went there,' he said abruptly. 'And my mother lived for the times he could come up, so when he died I bought the place for her.' His tone changed into pure cynicism. 'Besides, I owe him a lot, and he loved the place too.'

'You owe him?'

His smile was lethal. 'My father expected less of me than he did of his legitimate sons; it made me utterly determined to prove myself, so you could say my success is due to him.'

'I doubt it,' she returned crisply. 'You're like Gabe and Marco—a born leader.'

He said slowly, 'Thank you.'

Melissa said, 'Parents have such huge responsibilities, but I think people are born with their basic personalities pretty much fixed. Although my parents loved each other, it wasn't a comfortable marriage. I was too young to understand much about it, but my mother had affairs—she was so beautiful she drove men mad—and it hurt my father. Yet when he died she was inconsolable, and I'm sure that's what gave her cancer. She just didn't have the heart or the strength to fight it.'

He said, 'You said once that she left all of her money to your brothers, nothing to you. Why was that?'

'There actually wasn't much money in the end, but she expected my brothers to look after me. And once she told me that my father had married her for her money; he had very little after he was forced out of Illyria. She didn't want the same for me.' It was strangely sweet to be talking about their families, their backgrounds. The soft, fierce hum of passion was always there, but this was something else, a forging of bonds that were every bit as satisfactory as the wildfire hunger.

And even more dangerous. Because her heart was being so remarkably stubborn, she had to keep reminding herself that he was a man with no integrity when it came to sex.

'Do you think her affairs were a kind of punishment?'

'They might have been,' she said soberly. 'Poor Mama.'

His straight black brows lifted and, in a tone completely at variance with the keenness of his scrutiny, Hawke said, 'Nevertheless, she was remarkably unfair to you.'

'She was a little old-fashioned—men were meant to look after women, and all that.'

'Very out of date,' he agreed drily, a note in his voice making her wonder if he agreed with her mother.

'I wasn't the sort of daughter she wanted.' Damn! That had slipped out. In this mood he was too easy to confide in. She hastily adjusted her smile, allowing it to turn wry. 'I think she'd have liked a daughter with similar tastes, someone like Marie-Claire—they had a lot in common.'

'The glorious bride of last year?' He looked amused. 'Yes, your cousin is a glamorous creature, but it's all on the surface.'

Recalling the lavish, hugely romantic wedding a year ago, Melissa found herself wondering if Hawke had made love to Marie-Claire too.

Whatever, he'd certainly made love with Sara. Disillusion was an acrid taste in her mouth, a pain in her heart. She said curtly, 'What my mother got was a shy kid who spent most of her life with her nose in a book. It was an even bigger shock when I started to grow at twelve and towered above her within a year.'

Hawke sat down beside her. 'Didn't she realise you were going to be a beauty?'

Unease prickled through her; she disliked flattery. 'I know I'm not,' she said shortly. 'And if I've made her sound unkind, she wasn't—she did her best for me. She tried to give me the benefit of her superb taste, but it didn't "take"—I always knew that I'd never be like her.'

He frowned. 'You mean she criticised you all the time?'

'No, I do not!' she said swiftly, searching for a way to explain her mother and their relationship. 'She was trying to help—to give me the knowledge to become the sort of woman she was.'

'Did she know she was dying?'

'Yes. She'd told Gabe and Marco but she forbade them to tell me.' That still hurt. 'She sent me off to an English boarding-school. The first I knew about her illness was when Marco came to tell me she was dead.'

'She probably thought that would be easier for you than to stay at home and watch her die.'

'She didn't give me the choice,' Melissa said, old grief

leaching all colour and warmth from her voice. Over the years the raw sense of rejection inside her had eased into wry acceptance, but Hawke's words homed on to the last lingering remnant of resentment. 'I always thought it was because she loved my brothers much more than she loved me. They were everything she admired in a man—big and handsome and clever and very, very male. She adored them.'

'You said yourself that she was of the old school—allowing a child any say in her life might never have occurred to her,' he said objectively. 'Knowing that she hadn't long to live and that your brothers were busy men, she'd want you settled in a good school to give you some stability.'

Startled, she stared at him. His expression gave nothing away, yet for the first time she saw her mother through an adult's eyes—a woman facing her own mortality, knowing that Melissa would be alone in the world except for her brothers.

To her mother, looks and clothes had been all-important. She clearly hadn't realised that every comment to her adolescent daughter—acutely self-conscious about her height and her total lack of grace—chipped away at her fragile confidence.

If she'd lived, Melissa thought now, maybe they'd have come to an understanding denied them by her early death.

She blinked, fighting back tears at the chance death had filched from her. Hawke covered her hands with one of his, and something snapped inside her.

Green eyes speculative, he surveyed her. 'And you are beautiful.' His finger over her lips stopped her automatic objection. 'Oh, not in the conventional sense, perhaps.'

His fingertips skimmed a sweeping cheekbone. Rendered breathless by the bittersweet sensations spiralling through her body, Melissa listened to the rapid drumming of her heart, and thought despairingly, I love this man.

Desperately and without limit. Forever...

But love wasn't enough. She needed to be able to trust him.

'You wear your heritage in your face,' he said, an exciting rasp of tension in each word. 'These cheekbones were passed down by some horseman from the steppes, riding like doom through Europe. And your smouldering eyes probably came from the Caucasus—I wonder if some princess from the mountains brought them into your family?'

'Family legend says they're an inheritance from the queen who first owned the Queen's Blood.' Her words sounded faint and languishing.

'Ah, the famed rubies, so rare and exquisite they're priceless.' His eyelashes drooped. 'The only stones to suit your eyes would be diamonds from Australia, matched stone by stone to that exact gold. As for this satiny skin—perhaps the Saxon princess who bequeathed blue eyes to her male descendants left another heritage for the women who'd follow her.'

That tormenting finger stroked down Melissa's cheek, supercharging her rioting hormones so that she had to force herself to breathe.

Mercilessly, an odd little smile tucking in the corners of his sculpted mouth, he went on, 'I suspect that this very determined jaw is directly inherited from the first Considine of your house, and that you've also got his formidable stubbornness as well as his courage and will-power.'

Oh, he knew how to seduce! How often had he said similar things to the women he'd made love to? Yet when she looked into his eyes and saw the heat in their depths, her stomach endured an unnerving meltdown and all she could think of was that he might kiss her...

'As for your mouth,' he said softly, 'your mother probably

didn't even want to consider the fact that it's both sultry and innocent, passionate and eager and very addictive...'

Melissa's breath stopped in her lungs. She drowned in heated waves of desire, watched the words form on his hard lips and longed to kiss them into silence so that she could ignore the fragment of her brain that shouted a warning.

But he didn't bridge the final few centimetres between them.

'No,' he said with an ironic smile that cut into her dazed anticipation like a sword through honey, 'mothers of teenage girls don't want to think that one day they might grow up enough to find love and lose their hearts, and chart their futures away from their family.'

Melissa's heart stopped, then rebounded into erratic thudding. She searched his face as he got up and walked from the drowsy, rose-scented arbour into the warm, Mediterranean sunlight. It embraced him like a lover, showering him with gold.

Was he hinting at a *proposal*?

Of course not!

He was probably remembering that only a few hours ago they'd made love without protection, without even thinking of the risks. And that if by some chance she should be pregnant, his damned sense of responsibility meant he'd be saddled with her presence in his life, however irritating he found it.

Melissa tried to be grateful to him for stopping before they went too far, but her frustrated body howled common sense down, wanting only the surcease he could give her. One kiss, surely, wouldn't have been too much...

Oh, yes, it would!

'Would you like to swim?' he said, swinging around, his lean, handsome face sombre and forbidding.

Ever thoughtful, Marya had packed a bikini that made the most of Melissa's long legs and narrow waist, and entirely too much of her breasts. The thought of displaying herself in it made her skin tighten with eager urgency, but she refused sedately. 'No, thank you.'

'You've had a difficult day.' His tone was satiric, at odds with the keenness of his survey. 'Would you like to go inside out of the sun and rest?'

In that bedroom, so intimately close to his? Not likely.

Rising to her feet, she said with assumed brightness, 'I feel fine, and I'd like to see a bit more of the château grounds.'

After a moment he said courteously, 'Of course.'

They were as lovely as he'd promised, and when they came upon a *petanque* court he challenged her to a game.

Her heart jolted in her breast. 'I play to win,' she warned him. He grinned. 'Then let battle begin.'

Like her brothers, he made no concessions; neither did she. He beat her, but only just.

'You're good,' he said, his eyes measuring. 'Time for a drink; you've caught a little of the sun on the end of that aristocratic nose of yours. Come and sit down under the silk tree.'

He drank lime juice with her, the tangy flavour refreshing and stimulating even as the ice cubes cooled her down. Neither then, nor during the rest of the evening, did he offer her wine, or drink alcohol himself.

His deliberate abstention brought the possibility of pregnancy much too close.

And he left her at her bedroom door that night.

No doubt, she discovered a few moments later in her bathroom, because while they'd been eating dinner on a romantic, rose-laden terrace a package had been delivered to her room. Stomach churning, she read the instructions, and put the package down. Tomorrow morning she'd know for certain whether or not she carried Hawke's baby.

Melissa lay for hours until restlessness drove her across the dark room to a window. Out to sea lights twinkled; fishermen, perhaps, or one of the magnificent yachts at neighbouring Monaco, transporting its pampered passengers to another exotic destination.

Movement below caught her attention; she froze, devoutly thankful she hadn't turned on the lamp beside her bed. Hawke paced along the battlements, moving with the easy, lithe grace that was his alone, head slightly bent as though contemplating some difficult question.

What would he do if the test proved positive?

Melissa already knew she'd keep the child, but what would Hawke want? His family background made her uneasy; he would expect input into his child's upbringing.

And although her heart skipped a beat at the thought of keeping in contact, she knew such forced proximity would be hell. She drew the curtains with a swift jerk of her wrist, and turned away, cutting off Hawke's pacing figure.

She found the photograph in her bag and sat down on the bed. Could it be a fake? Squinting ferociously at it, she could find no signs of computer tampering. Anyway, the first thing Gabe would have done was have it checked by experts. And somewhere she'd read that it was almost impossible to falsify a photograph so that another computer couldn't discover the disconnections.

Gabe had accepted it as genuine; he'd broken his engagement to Sara within a week of receiving the shot.

Melissa could see why. She scanned the faces with cold, bitter envy. Hawke's arms held Sara, his expression one she'd never seen—much more tender and gentle. And Sara looked up at him, her lovely face urgent with entreaty, clearly begging him for sex.

Nausea roiled within her; she tasted the bitterness of betrayal. And that was stupid, because he'd made no promises to her…

Every time Hawke got too close, she'd force herself to remember this; in time she'd come to despise him.

But as she crawled back into the huge, lonely bed, her fingers lingered on her waist in an involuntary caress.

CHAPTER ELEVEN

MELISSA stared at the tiny stick with its blue band, and was assailed by pain so intense she couldn't hold back a soft moan as she sank onto the chair beside the bath.

Nothing. The knowledge echoed around her mind, ached through her body. There was no child, no excuse for keeping in touch with Hawke, no reason to hope.

She could go back to the Wolf's Lair, pick up her studies and force herself to continue with a life that stretched ahead in meaningless emptiness.

A knock on the door brought her to her feet. Sheer, brutal will-power stiffened her shoulders and wiped her face free of expression.

'Come in.'

And when Hawke entered she looked him straight in the eye and said baldly, 'There is no baby.'

When she saw the relief in his eyes she felt like screaming, but at least that was an honest reaction. Before he could say anything she hurried on, 'So I'll go home now.'

Still he didn't speak. Did he want proof? She waved the stick at him and said glibly, 'See for yourself.'

He didn't look at it. 'I won't say I'm sorry.'

I'm sorry, she thought savagely, hurting so much she

couldn't utter a word to fill the silence. I would have loved your baby and cared for it and been happy with it. But now there's no chance.

In a remote, hard voice that jolted her out of her pain, Hawke continued, 'I'm glad you're not pregnant because it's no way to start a marriage.'

Start a marriage? *Start a marriage!*

Her shocked gaze collided with his—stony and uncompromising. Baffled, she blurted, 'What on earth do you mean?'

The forceful framework of his face became even more prominent. 'You know perfectly well what I mean,' he said curtly. 'I'm asking you to marry me.'

A flash of incredulous delight was rapidly blotted out by bleak common sense. He didn't want marriage—he felt obliged to offer, probably because she was a Considine.

Torn by a combustible mixture of anger, grief and anguish, she dragged in a ragged breath and said in a voice entirely lacking any warmth or expression, 'I've just told you, there's no need to even think of marriage. There is no baby.' Pride drove her to finish rashly, 'Anyway, I wouldn't marry you if you were the last man on earth.'

Eyes glittering with temper, he said, 'I hope to be able to change your thinking on that.'

She tried to ward him off, but he ignored her fists and took her in his arms, crushing her against him as he kissed her.

It began fiercely, then transmuted into tenderness, and to her horror the brittle edifice of her control crumbled into shards, only to dissolve in the tears that stung her eyes.

She hiccuped and he tore his mouth from hers and stared into her eyes. 'Don't,' he ground out. 'Darling, don't cry, please.'

Terrified, Melissa wanted so much to give in—to what? A lifetime of wondering whose bed he was in? She didn't, she thought in aching despair, have the stamina for that. Better to make the break now, and make it clean and impossible to deny.

In a voice rough with emotion, she said, 'I have something to show you.'

He frowned, and his arms contracted around her until she said, 'Let me go.'

Reluctantly he did, waiting while she went across to the bureau. She fumbled in the drawer, eventually fishing out the photograph. Tension twisted inside her, but she held it out steadily, her face a proud, composed mask. She didn't dare speak; her voice would betray her.

Hawke took the photograph, but he didn't look at it straight away. Frowning, green eyes uncomfortably penetrating, he scrutinised her face. 'What is this?'

It took all of her self-possession to parry that unsparing, questing gaze with brittle composure. 'Look at it.'

Finally he looked down. Some cowardly part of Melissa— the part that wanted her to settle for a fool's paradise in his arms—demanded that she close her eyes. Defying it, she fixed her gaze on him in a wide, unblinking stare.

His face clamped into a forbidding mask. He looked up at her and said in a voice iced with barely controlled rage, 'What the *hell* is this?'

'A photograph of you and Sara Milton,' she told him unevenly. She clutched the back of the nearest chair and willed herself to stand upright, to meet the frozen fire of his gaze with every bit of pride and strength she could call to her aid.

'I know who she is.' He glanced down at the photograph again, his mouth a cruel line in the bold male contours of his face. 'So this is why you wouldn't stay in that room.'

'Yes,' she said, infusing her voice with bitter scorn. 'Check the time and date, Hawke.'

Eyes narrowing, he complied. She searched his face for shame, but there was nothing. Instead, his anger seemed transmuted into a leashed, predatory determination.

A shiver ran the length of Melissa's spine. He was looking at her as though she was prey, his eyes pure green and dangerous.

She said harshly, 'It was taken the night of Marie-Claire's wedding. The thought of sleeping in the bed where you made love with my brother's fiancée sickened me. Just as the thought of making love with you does now.'

His fingers clenched around the photograph, buckling it. 'Before you go any further,' he said with arrogant confidence, 'this is a fake.'

Melissa let her brows drift upwards in polite, implacable disbelief. 'And I suppose you didn't go into Sara's bedroom either.'

'I did,' he said, white around the mouth. 'Her maid had discovered that the Queen's Blood—you might remember she wore the rubies to Marie-Claire's ball that night—had disappeared from the safe. Sara was frantic.'

Steeling herself, Melissa said curtly. 'Nice try, but I don't believe you, Hawke. If they'd disappeared I'd have known about it. The Queen's Blood is still at the castle.'

He looked at her as though he hated her, eyes dark and hostile. 'It was gone—and only Sara and her maid knew the combination. I comforted Sara,' he said savagely. 'That's all— she was distraught with worry, and I put my arms around her and gave her a brotherly hug and told her we'd find it.'

'And of course the paparazzo took the photograph at just that moment. Unfortunately for your story, you don't look terribly brotherly to me,' Melissa pointed out politely, so angry and disappointed she could hardly articulate the words.

Very still, his expression calculating, he said softly, 'It's a fake, Melissa—a skilful one, I'll admit, but anyone with a good eye and a computer can shuffle body parts between people. Neither of us were naked, and the expressions on both faces have been altered.'

Melissa shut down the part of her that pleaded for her to accept his words. Gabe would have got an expert to check out the photograph, and if it had convinced him, then it couldn't have been manipulated.

Still in that coolly thoughtful voice, Hawke resumed, 'I'm beginning to wonder if this is a set-up. Did your brother realise he'd made a huge mistake after a few weeks of seeing his new fiancée operate in his world? Did he get rid of her in a way that would shut her up and make sure she didn't take him to court over such a summary dismissal? She brought a maid with her—who is now the housekeeper at the castle. What's her name…?'

'Marya,' Melissa supplied, shocked and disgusted by the ruthless workings of his mind. 'And she's honest.'

'I'm sure she is,' he said silkily, eyes narrowed and gleaming. 'Just as sure as I am that she's also Gabe's creature. You told me yourself, the valley people are intensely loyal to their ruling house. She'd do anything for him, even hide the rubies and come running to me, knowing I'd go with her to see what I could do. Your brother could have organised someone with a telephoto lens to be on hand in one of the trees in the garden, conveniently located for looking through the window—especially if the maid had pushed the curtain back.'

Melissa's head came up. 'No,' she said thinly, so outraged the hot words wouldn't come. 'No. Gabe wouldn't do that. Gabe would *never* do that.'

Shrugging, he said, 'Then there's nothing more to say, because I know this is a fake.'

He dropped the photograph onto the floor as though it contaminated his fingers. After a single contemptuous glance that pierced her heart, he turned his back and walked across to the door.

'Clearly you're convinced that I'd think nothing of sleeping with a friend's fiancée, so all this is a waste of time. I'll see that you're taken straight back to Illyria.' He looked at his watch. 'Be ready in an hour.'

Melissa watched the door close behind him and tried to tell herself that it was all for the best. She picked up the photograph and stared at it, quelling her nausea to give it another stringent survey.

Of course there were no signs of tampering.

Anyway, if by some remote chance he was right and it was a fake, there was still the brutal way he'd treated the actress, and Jacoba, his *very good friend* who obviously held a special place in his life.

Melissa lifted her chin. Her love was a jealous love; his unfaithfulness would kill her.

Yet he had a reputation for integrity...

'In business,' she said aloud, ignoring the pleading heart that was undermining her resolution.

She'd go back to her life and forget about him. He might want her, but wanting was easy and cheap. Love, she thought wearily, was much more difficult—it demanded so much. Absolute trust, for one thing, and absolute fidelity.

She couldn't trust him to be faithful.

And in spite of his honeyed words, she wasn't beautiful like Sara or Jacoba. What did she have to offer but a body that surrendered whenever he came to her?

Any other man she'd have suspected of wooing her to get close to her brothers, but Hawke didn't need that—he was his own man, matching her brothers in power and influence.

'Pity,' she said in a flat voice robbed of everything but the passionate need to go home, 'he doesn't match them in honesty.'

Hawke's farewell was delivered beside the car that took her to the airport; brief, formal and chillingly dispassionate, he wished her well, his expression controlled and his eyes hooded against her.

After returning stiff, conventional thanks for his hospitality, Melissa got into the car, her spine so rigid she thought that bending it might shatter her. She didn't look back as the car purred away from the château.

Her unnatural composure held until she was back in the Wolf's Lair, back in her room, back alone, as she'd be from now on for the rest of her life.

Even then she ignored Marya's fussing and managed to discipline her emotions. She slept, but in the middle of the night she woke from a dream of bleak disillusion to find herself sobbing, her body shaking with anguish, her throat aching as more sobs gathered.

Eventually sheer exhaustion silenced her, but for hours she lay watching the moon set over the mountains, her eyes burning and her heart a solid lump in her chest.

She would never see Hawke again, and she no longer had the fragile dream of his child to comfort her.

Stop wallowing, she commanded herself brutally. You're not the first person to fall in love and have it end badly, and you won't be the last. And it's not as though he loved you...

But why had he made such a dead set at her? Because she was a woman, and therefore desirable?

No. His previous lovers had all been utterly beautiful. Yet

from the first she'd been aware of his interest and the reciprocal sexual tug at her senses, a basic, earthy connection that bypassed the brain.

And, in Hawke's case, the eyes too, she thought grimly. Looking back, it had been there even when they danced together at Marie-Claire's wedding. She hadn't understood that simmering excitement, but he had.

And he'd decided not to act on it.

But when she'd proved herself so humiliatingly available in New Zealand, he hadn't been able to stop himself. Treacherous memory reminded her of his passion, of his intense, all-encompassing hunger...

For long minutes she let herself drift, her body heating as she recalled incidents—the way he cupped her breasts, the raw conviction in his voice when he told her she was beautiful. And his sensitivity each time they'd made love, the hot desperation of his hunger warring with an innate tenderness that made sure of her satisfaction rather than drive straight on to his own...

He *had* wanted her; he might have done nothing else for her, but he had taught her that she had it in her to be attractive to men.

But it still wasn't love, she told herself bitterly, and she wouldn't—couldn't!—be content with anything less.

A pity, then, that she didn't care about any man other than Hawke.

Her mouth tightened, but she blocked the tears. If she hadn't seen that photograph, what would she have done?

If he'd asked her to marry him, she'd have accepted.

Like a shot, she admitted tiredly, wishing her heart would give her some peace. She buried her face in the pillow. If only she could hide from the truth so easily...

She loved him.

Shivering, she got up and pulled on her robe before going

across to a window to look out across the valley her ancestors had fought for and cared for, and for which she and Gabe and Marco still felt a huge responsibility.

The mountains loomed into a sky hazed with stars, but her trickster mind superimposed another set of mountains—wilder, more primeval, cupping a lake, the air so fresh it almost hurt the lungs.

Two stops past the end of the world, Hawke had called Shipwreck Bay. She wished she'd never seen the place, never seen Hawke again, never discovered her own passionate nature—never lost her heart so irrevocably.

Because although she'd get over this agony of grief and betrayal, she knew she wouldn't be able to love anyone in the same way again.

'He's not worth it,' she muttered.

But oh, how she wished she hadn't seen the photograph!

The following day she guiltily slipped it back into Gabe's files. What would have happened if she'd accepted Hawke's proposal? Would Gabe have told her of Sara's betrayal?

Her brother was a fiercely private person—'And it's not going to happen, so why wonder?' she told herself bitterly. 'Forget about the whole sordid business.'

But for the next few days as she worked on the paper about her internship at Shipwreck Bay, her mind kept tripping her up with memories of Hawke—his tenderness, the way he made her laugh, his keen, fascinating mind—and she found herself making excuses for him.

Perhaps Sara had seduced him.

'If he's not strong enough—or trustworthy enough—to deal with temptation, why are you obsessing about him?' she asked aloud, staring through the window. The first snow—a light, almost inconsequential dusting—glittered like diamonds on the tops of the mountains, and the air coming through the open panes smelt of winter.

Like Shipwreck Bay, she thought, and her fingers hesitated on the computer keys as the memories surged back.

'Stop it!' she ordered, fixing her eyes on the valley, its ordered, bucolic charm so different from that untamed southern landscape—the landscape of her heart...

Angrily she blinked back the stinging tears. But although she could summarily dismiss her memories during the day, each night brought them flooding back, so vivid she lay twisting in her bed until exhaustion eventually dragged her under.

Each morning she forced herself up and down to breakfast, keeping her tormenting thoughts at bay with a magazine. The one the next morning almost held her attention until she came to an article—an interview with the actress who'd tried to kill herself after Hawke had dumped her.

Just what she needed—a reminder of how callous he could be. Melissa began to read it. After a few moments she dropped the magazine and said, 'No!'

Because Lucy St James was purporting to tell of another affront to her heart—and this time it was Marco Considine who'd broken it.

'I don't believe it!' Melissa muttered furiously, reading on with mounting outrage.

She finished the article, then went back and checked it. It was very cleverly done; there was plenty of flowery language, but nothing that could be checked except a glancing reference to an Easter rendezvous.

'Lies!' Melissa said, feeling sick. Apart from a couple of days spent with Alex and Ianthe and their family at the royal hunting lodge, Marco and she and Gabe had spent Easter at the castle, working out a plan for the valley.

She threw the magazine down onto the floor and covered her eyes.

Had the actress lied about Hawke too? After a moment's indecision, Melissa set her jaw and rang Marco.

'No,' he said firmly, his deep voice reassuring and utterly truthful. 'I did not have an affair with her. I've met her several times and turned down her far from subtle propositions, but she's as ambitious as hell. I suppose she needs publicity for this new film of hers, and the magazine was happy to oblige.'

Melissa digested this. 'What are you going to do?'

'Nothing,' he said calmly. 'It happens all the time, as you know, and I can't be bothered giving her more page space.'

When she'd hung up Melissa got up and walked across to the window. The broken heart the actress had blamed on Hawke had happened just after she'd landed a bit part in a high-profile film. It had been her big break.

So had she manufactured a story to attract attention? It seemed likely. Torn by a bewildering mix of relief and remorse, Melissa didn't know what to do.

'Nothing,' she said aloud slowly. Because she'd never accused Hawke to his face of shattering the woman's heart.

And the photograph was still there in its hideous accuracy.

Just before she was due back at university, her French cousin rang. 'Sweet, kind Melissa,' Marie-Claire said plaintively, 'I am alone and bored and pregnant. And sick! Come and stay with me until you go back to your dull studies.'

A humourless smile tucked in the corners of Melissa's mouth. 'Where are you?' she asked.

'At home, of course!' Marie-Claire and her husband lived in a palatial villa in the hills behind Nice. 'Do come, dearest one. My parents are in India and my darling is doing business in San Francisco and I am *so* tired of my own company.'

Melissa's wayward heart powered into overdrive. Stupid! She wasn't going anywhere near the Riviera—it was far too close to Hawke!

Opening her mouth to make some excuse, she stopped when Marie-Claire said quietly, 'I am lonely, Melissa.'

Hawke was probably back in New Zealand by now.

'All right,' she said, and listened to her cousin's extravagant thanks with a wry smile.

But Marie-Claire didn't look sick or lonely or pregnant. Radiant as always, she hugged Melissa with delight and accepted her congratulations with a brilliant smile.

'Come in,' she said, and eyed Melissa up and down. 'Oho, what has happened to you? You look ravishing! A little *triste*, but very, very chic. And you have been buying clothes! So, you must be in love!'

Trust Marie-Claire. Beneath the ditzy exterior lurked a shrewd Frenchwoman.

'I thought it was time I started to dress like a grown-up,' Melissa said in her most prosaic tone, already regretting the sudden impulse that had driven her to stop the car at one of the Riviera's most chic boutiques.

She'd splurged too much of her allowance on the darkly gold trousers that revealed her long legs and narrow hips, and a top that still felt scandalous, the white material subtly clinging to her breasts and dipping low to reveal more cleavage than she was comfortable with.

'Those sandals,' Marie-Claire crooned, drawing her into a small salon, 'look divine on you! And so sexy! You have such elegant ankles, and only someone as tall as you could get away with ankle straps! I approve!'

'Glad you do,' Melissa said woodenly.

Her cousin's eyes snapped with amusement. 'But I don't

think they were bought for me,' she said. 'And certainly not for your boring old university! Oh…' She whisked around to head out of the room. 'I have remembered something—I must attend to it immediately. Go outside and wait for me on the terrace.'

She closed the door behind her, and, somewhat bewildered, Melissa walked to the sunny terrace outside.

Tall, dark and dominating, a figure moved out of the shadows beneath the vine, and into the light.

CHAPTER TWELVE

MELISSA froze, her pulse rate increasing exponentially. She knew immediately who it was—and some unregenerate part of her was secretly delighted she'd bought new clothes.

After one glance at Hawke's implacable face she whispered hoarsely, 'What are you doing here?'

'Meeting you in a neutral place,' he said, his inflexible voice abrading her taut nerves.

'I'll kill Marie-Claire.'

His uncompromising mouth twisted in mockery. 'Don't blame her—I'd have engineered this meeting without her if I'd had to. There's no place you can go that I won't find you.' He waited for his words to sink in before finishing, 'So you might as well stay and listen to what I have to say.'

She started to protest, but he cut her off ruthlessly. 'If you decide that you don't believe me, I'll never bother you again.'

Nervously she wet her lips. 'I… All right,' she said reluctantly, hoping she could withstand the urgent demands of her heart—and the freshly wakened appetite of her senses.

His smile turned savage. 'Don't look so harassed. I won't touch you.'

Colour stung her cheeks. 'Just get on with it.'

He turned his head in autocratic summons, and a man materialised from the dark shade of a bay tree.

Melissa frowned, for as the newcomer came closer she thought she recognised him, only to dismiss that idea. There was nothing memorable about his features, nothing to fix him in the mind; eminently forgettable, he was the epitome of an inconspicuous person.

'Meet Brent Thomas,' Hawke said in a voice without inflection. 'He's a photographer.'

Brent Thomas met her intent stare with a cocky smile that morphed into a poker face after an uneasy glance at Hawke.

Stonily she said, 'I see.'

'I suppose you do,' the photographer said, ducking his head. He spoke with a mid-Atlantic accent, his voice slightly nasal. 'I took the shot of Mr Kennedy and Ms Milton in his château.'

He held out a photograph. Stunned, Melissa took it, intending to allow herself a swift, distasteful glance. Her brows drew together as she examined it more closely, and her heart quickened.

It was like—and yet so different from—the one in Gabe's files. Sara and Hawke were in the same position—his arms around her, her face lifted to his—but in this shot both were clothed; Hawke was fully dressed in T-shirt and trousers, Sara Milton wearing a wrap.

And the faces had been subtly altered. Instead of gazing at each other in open lust, Hawke looked concerned and Sara was clearly fighting back tears.

Hope pumped through Melissa, but she didn't dare accept it. 'This isn't the real one,' she stated in her most matter-of-fact tone.

After another glance at Hawke, Brent Thomas said hastily, 'It's the real one.'

'I don't believe you.' She didn't dare look at Hawke so she kept her eyes on the photographer's face, wincing internally when saw him hesitate.

Brent Thomas said, 'Well, it's a matter of trust, isn't it? And if I say so myself, I did a good job.'

Hawke's iron-hard voice broke into his private congratulatory moment. 'Get on with it.'

The photographer sent him a harried glance before saying, 'Just ask yourself—which one is going to get me the most money?'

He had a point. She glanced at the photograph again. 'Someone could have paid you to alter it.'

He gave a wry smirk. 'Not likely. Your brother, now, he paid up because he didn't want to look a fool.' His face darkened. 'Mind you, he made sure I won't work again, ever. He plays rough, Gabe Considine.'

'If this photograph was altered to the one I saw, you deserved it,' she said curtly.

Her contempt must have stung. He said heatedly, 'What would you know—never had to do a hand's tap of work in your life, never known—?'

'That's enough.' Hawke's interjection lifted the hairs on the back of Melissa's neck.

The photographer subsided, somehow shrinking. 'All right.' He glanced from Hawke's hard, intimidating face to Melissa. 'Mr Kennedy, he hasn't paid me a penny. No, he just threatened to go to the police.'

He swallowed, and Melissa realised that beneath the surly surface he was afraid. 'Go on.'

'This whole business has taught me a lesson. Don't muck the rich around. They don't like it. You think paparazzi are scum? Well, perhaps we push things a bit, but I can tell you we don't go round threatening people and pulling strings so other people lose their jobs.'

Hawke said in that same quiet, deadly voice, 'Selling photographs is one thing—altering them to use for blackmail is another. You have no idea of the misery you caused. Why did you do it?'

'I had no choice,' he muttered. 'My kid was sick. She needs treatment, and I didn't have the money.'

'Why?' Hawke asked sternly.

Brent Thomas sent him a furtive look, then turned to Melissa, instinctively appealing, she thought with aversion, to the person he judged the easier to con. 'All right, so I gambled it. But I didn't know my kid was sick. Her mother ran out on me.'

'You chose a man with a deep pocket and hoped you could bleed him without getting caught,' Hawke said, his voice cold and authoritative. 'Don't expect any sympathy from either of us. Before you get the hell out of here, what else do you have to say?'

Shuffling his feet, Brent Thomas muttered, 'Only that I'm sorry I caused you any pain.'

Melissa asked, 'How is your little girl now?'

The photographer gave her an astonished look, then flushed. 'She's good, so far. The tumour was benign, but it might grow again even though the surgeon says he got it all. It was in her brain, you see.'

Melissa opened her mouth, but Hawke overrode her offered sympathy with a forceful lack of finesse. 'Get out,' he said icily. 'If you ever try anything like this again you'll end up in gaol, sick child or no sick child.' He paused before finishing in a tone that sent a shudder down Melissa's spine, 'And I'll know. From now on, watch your back.'

The photographer turned and blundered out into the warm

autumn sun. Melissa watched as another man stamped with a security guard's authority escorted him away.

She stared at the photograph, innocent and unsullied by trickery, and asked numbly, 'Was it all true, then? Did the Queen's Blood really get stolen?'

Hawke said, 'It was true.' He paused, then added in an expressionless voice, 'I believe it's been found again.'

She had to swallow to ease her dry throat. 'I see,' she said colourlessly. And because she couldn't think of anything else to say, she whispered, 'I'm so sorry.'

'You have nothing to be sorry about.'

He sounded very distant and completely fed up. Utterly wretched, Melissa didn't blame him. She cast about in her mind for words to convince him of her regret, but one glance at his stony face told her it would be wasted effort.

Instead, she said, 'I understand that he was desperate, but I wonder if he has any remorse at all for the harm he's done.'

'Very little,' Hawke said coolly. 'And his desperation was entirely his own fault. No one forced him to gamble his very hefty income away. He sees us as legitimate prey; we have money, power, position—all the things he'd like to have but doesn't want to work for. Don't waste your sympathy on him.'

Well, she'd always known Hawke was ruthless.

Chilled, she said, 'Gabe! We have to tell Gabe that he faked the photos! It might not be too late for him to make up with Sara!'

When Hawke laughed she raced across to him and seized his arm, shaking it indignantly. 'I mean it—you didn't see him after he broke it off with her. Hawke, we have to tell him!'

'I think he already knows,' Hawke said, reaching into his pocket to haul out a creased piece of newspaper. 'Go on, take it.'

Too bewildered to do anything but obey, she unfolded it.

It was a photograph of two people walking hand in hand along a tropical beach. One was Gabe and the other—

'It's Sara,' Melissa breathed, so astonished she barely got the words out.

'Read it,' Hawke said.

'On Again?' the headline read.

Prince Gabriele Considine, Grand Duke of Illyria, walking along a tropical beach with his former fiancée Sara Milton. Looks as though the rift in the lute was only temporary. Another royal wedding in Illyria soon?

Unable to believe her eyes, Melissa switched her astonished look to Hawke's amused face. 'Where—how did you get this?' she asked faintly.

'It came out in one of the tabloids this morning—my PA made sure I read it. They're on an island called Fala'isi in the Pacific.'

'Sara spent her childhood there.' Melissa smiled, a rush of delight for Sara and Gabe overwhelming all the questions she still had. 'Oh, that's wonderful! I liked her so much.'

'Good,' Hawke said forcefully, and hauled her into his arms and kissed her with frankly sensual enjoyment.

Melissa's bones melted; she kissed him back with as much fire and passion, as much of the intense yearning and love she could produce.

'All right,' he said when they finally had to breathe, 'I've had enough of this. I will ask you only once more to marry me.'

Happiness exploded inside her like fireworks, incandescent, as brightly coloured as her future. But there were still a couple of dark clouds in her sky.

Extricating herself from him, she ask quietly, 'Why did you propose when you discovered there wasn't a baby?'

'Because I couldn't help myself,' he said bluntly. 'I didn't want there to be a child then—no, hell, I'd have been delighted to find that you were pregnant! I knew you'd never marry me just because you were pregnant. And a shotgun marriage isn't want I wanted for us.'

'You're right,' she said, her defensive stance relaxing a little. 'But what about Jacoba Sinclair?'

His eyes darkened dangerously. 'What about her? I thought I'd convinced you—'

'She was hurt when she found me at your bach.'

'Not hurt,' he said, a thread of iron in his tone, 'but shocked. And I'm sorry, but I can't tell you why. I promised her I wouldn't, and I don't go back on my promises. That applies to the vows I hope to make to you at our wedding.' He paused, his face suddenly grim and proud. 'I can't prove that we were never lovers. You must decide whether or not to believe me when I say that I'll never be unfaithful to you.'

Melissa searched his unyielding face. She felt as though she was on the edge of a precipice, terrified and unable to move. Yet she had to either fall, or fly. To believe him was such an act of trust—could she do it?

She said, 'You didn't dump Lucy St James, did you?'

His expression darkened. 'That too?' he asked savagely. 'No. We only met a couple of times.'

A tight knot inside Melissa started to unravel at last, and with it went her instinctive need to keep him at a distance. Wonderingly, she said, 'I think I only believed it because I thought it would keep me safe. I was so scared of falling in love with you.'

He gave a hard crack of mirthless laughter. 'Both of us. Do you think I wanted to fall in love with you? You're too young, too—too *much*.' He ran a hand through his thick hair and glowered at her. 'I planned on getting married, of course, but it was going to be safe and controllable—nothing like this wild demolition of every barrier until I'm naked and utterly consumed by need for you.'

Her heart twisted. 'Yes,' she said simply. 'No safety net at all. It's terrifying.'

'And glorious.' He gave another crack of laughter. 'God, you've put me through hell.'

'It was entirely mutual,' she said drily.

He sobered instantly. Eyes glittering and fierce, he said quietly, 'There will be times when we are apart; there will be times when the media print heavily slanted gossip. I want to marry you, Melissa, but I have to know you trust me, because distrust poisons, it erodes love, it kills hope and faith and desire. If you can't trust me, then tell me now and let's end it. I can't force it; you have to give it freely.'

She gazed at his beloved face, and saw the truth. Hawke was looking at her with such intense possessiveness, such fierce pleasure—and a naked, stripped longing that tore at her heart.

She peeped soulfully through her lashes at him. 'Ask me to marry you again—oh, you said you wouldn't! Not even if it's third time lucky?'

His eyes glimmered with laughter. 'Not even then. I always keep my promises. But I'm sure I can find some interesting way of extracting a promise from you without actually asking for it…'

Mischief glinted like gold diamonds in her eyes. He watched as she picked up the hem of an imaginary balldress and swept him an elaborate formal court curtsey that ended in her gracefully sweeping almost to the floor. She paused for a few graceful seconds, and then rose.

Demurely she said, 'I am *so* looking forward to that. Hawke, will you marry me, please?'

'Yes.'

'Just like that?' She gazed at him in mock disappointment. 'Perhaps you should think about it—or I might need to persuade you—?'

'I don't need to think, and you could probably persuade me to jump off a cliff,' he said, and hauled her into his arms again. He stared into her face with hot, fierce eyes. 'You exquisite torment! I've thought about nothing else for weeks—in fact, it was after I met you at Marie-Claire's wedding that I decided it was probably time to look for a wife. Not that I admitted it! But meeting you at Shipwreck Bay seemed like a gift from the gods. I'll love you for the rest of my life.'

'And I will love you,' she said blissfully.

'You'd better,' he threatened, hugging her against his lean, aroused body. 'Because I won't let you go.' He lifted her chin and looked down into her eyes. 'I must have fallen in love with you when we danced together at Marie-Claire's wedding, but I don't think I even believed in love then, certainly not love at first sight. But I found myself buying up diamonds the exact colour of the gold glitter in your eyes, and when we met again at Shipwreck Bay it was all over for me.'

'I'm sorry.' Her whole being exulting, she burrowed into him. 'I fell in love with you then, but it was too quick, too—well, you said it, just too much, like being hit by a meteor!' She leaned back, eyes devouring his beloved face, her heart so full she loved everyone in the world, even, she thought dreamily, the sleazy, whining photographer who'd caused so much trouble. 'But I'd read about you—about your gorgeous lovers and Jacoba apparently always waiting patiently in the wings, and then about Lucy St James and her suicide attempt.'

'*Supposed* suicide attempt,' he said, his voice hard. He

kissed her eyelids closed and said in a different voice, 'Do you believe that Jacoba and I were never lovers?'

'Yes,' she said quietly, her heart light now that it was freed from its burden of distrust.

'I can't tell you why she came to me at the bach, but I can tell you that she's the daughter of an old friend of my mother's.' He paused, his brows drawing together, his eyes darkly penetrating. 'There are reasons why she doesn't want her background known. I can't tell you, I'm afraid.'

She looked at him and read nothing but integrity in his expression. 'It's all right,' she said quietly. 'I'd probably have believed you if I hadn't found the photograph.'

'I understand.' Hawke kissed her again. A long time later, he said, 'You found it while I was at the Wolf's Lair, didn't you.'

It was a statement, not a question. Melissa nodded and turned her face into his throat. The silken, slightly abrasive texture of the skin along his determined jaw sent shivers of delighted response through her.

She explained how she'd come across the photo, adding in a voice bleak with remembered grief, 'I wanted to die.'

'Your loyalty to Gabe does you honour,' he said with an odd formality that caught at her heart.

She looked up and said honestly, 'It wasn't just that— although it hurt to think you'd made love to my brother's fiancée. I love you so much that the thought of you wanting anyone else hollows me out inside and makes me bitter with jealousy. I couldn't cope with an unfaithful husband, Hawke. It would kill me. So I thought I was saving myself from pain by rejecting you.'

He released her, but only to cup her face with his lean hands and hold her gaze with his own. In a smoky voice, deep and raw, he said, 'I love you utterly, with everything in me, with all my heart and soul. There's no room in my heart or my life for anyone else. I won't betray you—but I need the same from you. I need you to trust me, Melissa, as I trust you.'

'I do,' she promised. 'I'm planning to trust you with my happiness—doesn't that tell you something?'

He dropped his hands and stood back, his narrowed eyes burnished and gleaming. 'God knows, I've tried to be restrained where you're concerned, but I can't be. I'm utterly and wholly besotted with you, and I'll spend the rest of my life making you happy.'

He spoke the words like a vow, a solemn, quiet, deeply intense affirmation that satisfied the final murmurings of her hungry heart.

Voice shaking with the force of her emotions, she said, 'I'll make you happy, I promise.'

He looked down into her eyes and kissed her, a gentle kiss that sealed their commitment.

When Marie-Claire came peeping around the door they were still locked in each other's arms, in wordless contentment and peace at having at last found each other.

'So,' she said, glowing with mischief, 'you are both happy now? You are engaged to be married?'

They smiled at her and said, 'Yes,' together.

Suddenly serious, she said, 'Then we have plans to make. Hawke, this will be no ordinary wedding, you understand. Alex, as Prince of Illyria and head of the house of Considine, must be told. But first you need to contact Gabe and ask him for permission to address his sister.'

Flushing and horrified, Melissa said, 'Oh, Marie-Claire— that's not necessary!'

But Hawke released her. 'Damn! I assume you're talking about an official wedding?'

Marie-Claire laughed. 'Of course,' she said cheerfully. 'I think you will find that Prince Alex will decide to celebrate it with all the pomp and ceremony he can manage. The poor Illyrians have had little enough to enjoy for the past fifty years. Apart from murdering everyone who opposed him, the dictator played each region against the other, so Alex is keen to give them some sort of unity. Weddings are a universal joy.'

Hawke glanced at Melissa. She said with resignation, 'She's right, I'm afraid.'

Marie-Claire smiled sympathetically at Hawke's arrogant face. 'I'm afraid that people who marry into royal families are used unmercifully for official reasons, which is why I'm glad that I'm not a Considine. But Melissa is, and she is now a princess of Illyria, so everything must be done with the Illyrians in mind.'

For the first time Hawke understood that he'd always share her with the Illyrians. Ruthlessly controlling his urge to send every last one of her countrymen to hell and marry her out of hand, he demanded, 'And how long does it take to organise an official wedding?'

Marie-Claire looked sympathetic. 'About as long as it takes to organise any large wedding,' she said demurely. 'At least a year.'

Hawke bit back words that were better left unsaid. He looked at Melissa, obviously as dismayed as he was, and his whole being rose in revolt.

And then he said calmly, 'All right, we can do that.'

His love turned a wrathful face towards him, and he dropped a kiss on her soft mouth, more to silence her than to reassure her.

Marie-Claire said brightly, 'Of course, that is the *official* wedding.' She smiled benignly at them both. 'And now I have decided to join my husband for a few days, so the villa is yours.'

Later that night, almost asleep, Melissa said on a long, satisfied sigh, 'How on earth are we going to wait for a year? We won't be able to openly live together, you know—the Illyrians are pretty strict about morals.'

Hawke's chest lifted and she felt, rather than heard, his soft laughter. 'I'll negotiate the time span back to six months,' he said easily. 'But in New Zealand you can get married within three days…'

She lifted her head and surveyed him, loving the chance to openly show her feelings. He lay sprawled across the white sheets like some sleek, sated predator, bronze hide glowing in the dim light, relaxed as she'd never seen him before. And even as the dark fire began to burn again in the depths of his eyes, she knew that she had done this for him—that he loved her.

Thanking whatever gods had given her this, she bent her head and kissed one muscular shoulder. 'A private wedding on the beach?' she whispered. 'I'd love that if we can do it, but really, nothing matters now that I know you love me. We'll work things out. Only…'

He captured a roving hand and held it against his heart. 'Only?' he prompted.

'Will you mind that sometimes—like the official wedding—we'll have to consult Alex? And I want to finish my degree, and then I did want to work out a tourism project for the valley and, if that's a success, for Illyria. I'll always feel that I owe them whatever I can give them.'

He lifted her hand to his lips and kissed it, her fingers and the soft palm. 'Your loyalty is one of the things I love about you,' he said deeply. 'And I couldn't bear to offer you a marriage that takes away from you, rather than adds to your life. You'll do whatever you want to; we both have responsibilities and we'll have to make compromises, but not too many.'

Melissa kissed him again. 'I love you so much,' she said, her heart swelling.

'And I love you—forever.'

She eased herself down, and listened to the steady beat of his heart beneath her ear. From now on, she thought as she drifted off to sleep in his arms, they were where they were meant to be—safe with each other.

*They're the men who have
everything—except brides...*

Wealth, power, charm—what else could a heart-stoppingly
handsome tycoon need? In the GREEK TYCOONS miniseries
you have already been introduced to some gorgeous
Greek multimillionaires who are in need of wives.

Now it's the turn of favorite Presents author

Lynne Graham,

with her attention-grabbing romance...

RELUCTANT MISTRESS, BLACKMAILED WIFE

On sale November 2006.

This tycoon has met his match, and he's decided
he has to have her...whatever it takes!

www.eHarlequin.com

HPGT1106

Even more passion for your reading pleasure!

Escape into a world of intense passion and scorching
romance! Everything you've always loved in
Harlequin Presents books, but we've turned up
the thermostat just a little, so that the relationships
really sizzle....

Kimberley's little boy is in danger, and the only person
who can help is his father. But Luc doesn't even know
his son exists. The gorgeous Brazilian tycoon will help—
provided Kimberley sleeps with him....

MILLION-DOLLAR LOVE-CHILD

by Sarah Morgan

Available November 2006.
Don't miss it!

www.eHarlequin.com

HPUC1106

SAVE UP TO $30! SIGN UP TODAY!

INSIDE *Romance*

The complete guide to your favorite
Harlequin®, Silhouette® and Love Inspired® books.

✓ Newsletter ABSOLUTELY FREE! No purchase necessary.

✓ Valuable coupons for future purchases of Harlequin,
Silhouette and Love Inspired books in every issue!

✓ Special excerpts & previews in each issue. Learn about all
the hottest titles before they arrive in stores.

✓ No hassle—mailed directly to your door!

✓ Comes complete with a handy shopping checklist
so you won't miss out on any titles.

- -

SIGN ME UP TO RECEIVE INSIDE ROMANCE
ABSOLUTELY FREE
(Please print clearly)

Name

Address

City/Town   State/Province   Zip/Postal Code

(098 KKM EJL9)

Please mail this form to:
In the U.S.A.: Inside Romance, P.O. Box 9057, Buffalo, NY 14269-9057
In Canada: Inside Romance, P.O. Box 622, Fort Erie, ON L2A 5X3
OR visit http://www.eHarlequin.com/insideromance

IRNBPA06R   ® and ™ are trademarks owned and used by the trademark owner and/or its licensee.

If you enjoyed what you just read,
then we've got an offer you can't resist!

Take 2 bestselling love stories FREE!
Plus get a FREE surprise gift!

Clip this page and mail it to Harlequin Reader Service®

IN U.S.A.
3010 Walden Ave.
P.O. Box 1867
Buffalo, N.Y. 14240-1867

IN CANADA
P.O. Box 609
Fort Erie, Ontario
L2A 5X3

YES! Please send me 2 free Harlequin Presents® novels and my free surprise gift. After receiving them, if I don't wish to receive anymore, I can return the shipping statement marked cancel. If I don't cancel, I will receive 6 brand-new novels every month, before they're available in stores! In the U.S.A., bill me at the bargain price of $3.80 plus 25¢ shipping & handling per book and applicable sales tax, if any*. In Canada, bill me at the bargain price of $4.47 plus 25¢ shipping & handling per book and applicable taxes**. That's the complete price and a savings of at least 10% off the cover prices—what a great deal! I understand that accepting the 2 free books and gift places me under no obligation ever to buy any books. I can always return a shipment and cancel at any time. Even if I never buy another book from Harlequin, the 2 free books and gift are mine to keep forever.

106 HDN DZ7Y
306 HDN DZ7Z

Name	(PLEASE PRINT)	
Address	Apt.#	
City	State/Prov.	Zip/Postal Code

Not valid to current Harlequin Presents® subscribers.

Want to try two free books from another series?
Call 1-800-873-8635 or visit www.morefreebooks.com.

* Terms and prices subject to change without notice. Sales tax applicable in N.Y.
** Canadian residents will be charged applicable provincial taxes and GST.
   All orders subject to approval. Offer limited to one per household.
   ® are registered trademarks owned and used by the trademark owner and or its licensee.

PRES04R   ©2004 Harlequin Enterprises Limited

He's proud, passionate, primal—
dare she surrender to the Sheikh?

Feel warm winds blowing through your hair
and the hot desert sun on your skin as you are transported
to exotic lands…. As the temperature rises, let yourself be
seduced by our sexy, irresistible sheikhs.

Available this November.

With a brooding stranger, Zara Kingston finds the
Zaddara desert holds hidden treasures.
But what happens when Zara discovers the stranger
is Sheikh Shahin…thief of her youth!

BEDDED BY THE
DESERT KING

by Susan Stephens

**On sale November 2006.
Get your copy today!**

www.eHarlequin.com   HPSTS1106

HARLEQUIN Presents

**Celebrate Christmas
with one of your favorite
Harlequin Presents authors!**

THE SICILIAN'S CHRISTMAS BRIDE
by Sandra Marton

On sale November 2006.

When Maya Sommers becomes Dante Russo's
mistress, rules are made. Although their affair
will be highly satisfying in the bedroom,
there'll be no commitment or future plans.
Then Maya discovers she's pregnant....

Get your copy today!

www.eHarlequin.com   HPSCB1106